# THAW

## ROBERT FENWICK MAY, JR

**Thaw**

Written by: Robert Fenwick May, Jr.

Formatted by: eDesk Services
Edited by Angelo Reid.
Cover art by Seth Amoako Kena.

Print ISBN: 9798375034089

# DEDICATION

*For Savanah,*
*my bestest bud.*

"Everything we call real is made of things that cannot be regarded as real."

NIELS BOHR

# PROLOGUE

FETU HELD the orb in his hands, his long fingers wrapping around it. It pulsed with life. He could feel the thrumming of it in his very core. It was beautiful in the light of the full moon and shown like the mother of pearl. He ran his finger over it slowly, almost caressing it. It was reflected in his large black almond-shaped eyes like it was his iris. The orb was perfectly round and full of life. It crackled with energy. He stood at the top of the tower as the wind whipped through his robe. It was a cool day, but not chilly. The air was fresh and clean. He could smell the ocean, the salt tingling his nose ever so slightly. He slowly walked toward the black obelisk pedestal that stood at the tower's center.

Once this was done, there was no turning back.

He knew that he was the last of his kind. He had lived alone too long and could feel the end was near. Eons had passed since he had last seen a loved one. Even more time had passed since he had seen anyone at all. His loneliness was deeper than anything he could bear. The tower had been built just for this purpose. His people had known that they would not last forever. No civilization does. None have. They knew moving meditatively. Each footfall was deliberate. He touched his heel and then rolled off the toe to gently place the other heel down, timing his breath with each step. He was deeply in the gamma brain wave state. He was one with everything around him. His consciousness reached the limits of the universe. He was the center of an endless cosmos.

The meteor was coming. There was no stopping it. It would change everything. It would cover the Earth in a nuclear winter. The time had come. The planet had passed through the tail of the comet.

Slowly he made his way to the center of the platform, The pedestal was blacker than any quantum singularity, so black that light did not escape it. He looked into it as he slowly and deliberately approached, gazing into infinity.

As he came closer to the pedestal, the orb was being tugged from him. It had begun, the beginning of his end. There was no stopping it now. The orb carried everything, and once he released it, he would pass on all that it carried... not knowing who the information would ultimately reach, if anyone at all. All the knowledge of his kind, all of the science and art and culture, his very existence slipped from his fingers. What was left behind was paramount.

It was time. He felt his soul being tugged along with it, slowly leaving his body and entering the orb as it moved toward the pedestal. For a brief moment, he felt outside himself, observing this scene he had imagined so many times and was now part of. He could see his outstretched hands as they hovered in mid-air. The orb was ready, tugging his hands, ready to be released. Fetu relaxed his fingers, allowing the orb to gravitate upwards. As the device moved, his consciousness moved with it. His body had served him well but was now a husk he could leave behind; his mind was now within the orb. Together they reached their destination.

The orb floated to the top of the pedestal and hovered over the depression at the top of it for a brief moment. It buzzed and crackled with energy. The pedestal had begun thrumming deeply. Suddenly it snapped into place the way strong magnets attract each other. A brilliant flash of light emanated and completely illuminated the surrounding land like noon in the desert. Animals, small and large, turned to look, and for a minute, all was still. Then the tower sealed itself with an incredible clap louder than any thunder heard on Earth. The ground shook. The shock wave rippled around the entire globe. The orb was locked in place upon its throne for all eternity.

The force of the closure expelled Fetu's empty shell of a body outward. Slowly it fell to the Earth down the side of the tower, limp and lifeless in the deafening silence. It didn't make a sound as it tumbled end over end to its final destination. The Tower flared out at its base. It was as wide as it was tall, completely smooth. His body slid down the side gently.

The entire planet was quiet for a few moments after he came to rest at the bottom of the tower. The wind blew again and a single leaf somer-saulted by... painfully, the world restarted. The tower stood perfectly still and strong and smooth and sealed. At the base of the tower, the faint hint of a moving hieroglyph emerged and was gone.

In the distance, the beginnings of a bright streak started to emerge in the night sky.

# CHAPTER ONE

THE EARTH CONTINUED TO WARM, and the ice continued to melt. Water levels rose, and the cities flooded. The entire Earth became a Venice, awash with liquid. Amazingly, people didn't flee the cities as was expected. There were total losses, such as Key West and San Francisco. If the city had tall buildings, they stood and were used. Some did, of course, move towards the center of the land, but most stayed. Boat owners turned into Uber drivers. Humans adapted, moving the many devices that support our lives — heating, cooling, and electrical systems, all had been in the flooded basements, so they were moved to the roofs. Buildings kept functioning

Boats that had once seemed frivolous or luxurious now became essential. Instead of traffic jams, the streets became waterways. The pizza was still delivered. Accidents still happened. Work went on in the office buildings. Outside the cities, adapting was harder in places with less elevation, such as the midwest.

Countless towns were lost in the flood. Large cities such as New Orleans and coastal towns such as N.C. Outer Banks, Cape Cod, and Atlantic City... were all lost early, doomed by their low elevation. We tried, of course, to hold back the water. Levis broke, dams burst or were overrun, becoming useless. This left little land to live on. We used what was left. Mountain homes had become of great value.

The entire Earth's ecosystem suffered... water currents and temperatures changed, reefs died, and mass extinctions of fish and mammals alike. As Antarctica melted, it became a dry continent instead of the glacier haven it had been. Of course, the freshwater flood was a disaster. Currents changed, and along with it, the weather.

The Antarctic ice shelf holds about 26.5 million cubic kilometers of ice, and N.O.A.H. had predicted it would cause sea levels to rise 19 to 20 stories high if it melted. The water rose to 15 stories, so N.O.A.H.'s estimates were close.

Ocean life dwindled as people relied on the sea for food. While much land was submerged and lost to the sea, in places, other land emerged. As Antarctica melted, it became a dry continent instead of the glacier haven it had been.

The drying of Antarctica had created a new landmass that attracted new life and people as it became its own ecosystem in the warming climate. Ice at the north pole was a thing of the past. So much for Santa's workshop. Life goes on. We adapt and overcome.

Hydroponic gardening developed into the sexy new science and answer to feeding the masses. Scuba diving lessons skyrocketed. eBay was replete with artifacts found on the bottom in dangerous places only the very brave or foolhardy dared go in the dark, cold depths of basements and storage containers.

The Earth did not completely become a water world. The land still existed. There was just... less of it. Man-made floating cities were our new tech innovations. Humans continued to develop solar and wind power. It wasn't a lawless free-for-all. The United States Navy still had command of the oceans. Governments still functioned, and the law still existed. The police still did their jobs. People still went to work, had families, and planned for the future. Granted, with less land, the planet was more crowded. Most had lost someone, many of those to floods, starvation, drowning, or waterborne illnesses in the early years. Half of the population died as it adjusted to the new norm.

What wasn't expected was what the thawing ice sheets revealed. When Antarctica became an inhabitable landmass, it revealed under the thawed ice a giant tower smack dab in the middle of it. If there had been a civilization surrounding it, it was long gone. The tower stood cold, dark, and impenetrable. When was it built? There was no way to carbon date it. Did they have a culture, language, or distinct architecture? Did aliens put it there? Was it a past human civilization? Humans that have been here on Earth, living in Antarctica, with much more advanced technology than we currently have? Questions raged, and theories were debated.

The biggest problem was that it was completely smooth and closed off. Not a single opening or seam could be found on it. We had no idea how to open it and explore the technology inside. Not yet, anyway, maybe the scientists will find a way the news anchors mused. For now, the tower stood just as a curiosity in the howling wind. We couldn't get inside the complex to see who or what the creators were.

All of the world's countries were interested in it, each convinced that some advanced weaponry lay within. Maybe some technology would help them make a new weapon, or minerals or other riches that could be sold to make weapons... you get the idea. Despite the flood, politics was still politics, and countries continued their quest to be the first, the richest, and the most powerful. Slowly each nation-state staked out territory around the tower's base and began to study it.

A small United Nations of scientists from different countries were drawn to Antarctica and the mystery of the tower. All bent on studying the tower itself and how to open it. Some tried to drill into the side of it, but this proved fruitless. Nothing could scratch it. The material it was made of was of unknown properties.

Scientists need to eat, and they need supplies, which caused a small city to form around the scientists' bases. Each country also sent in the military to guard their 'turf,' and those in uniform also needed food. They also need entertainment. Thus grew a shanty town that took on a life of its own. It was abuzz with life and already developing its own culture.

# CHAPTER TWO

WHEN THE FIRST signs of the tower appeared, the internet went berserk. Only a third of Antarctica had melted in those early days, so the very top of the tower began to show. Debates over what it was were extremely intense. It started like all unexplained phenomena on the internet. Fuzzy Google Earth pictures of Antarctica and conspiracy theorists saying, "What is this? An alien artifact?" Speculations ran from a government secret base to ancient alien tech finally being revealed due to the thaw. As time progressed and more showed, it became apparent that it wasn't just a trick of shadow or a dark boulder being exposed. There was something there. Depending on your view, something huge and unlike anything else on earth.... Mysterious, magical, unexplainable, or alien.

Despite the media frenzy that followed, most people were not surprised to find an alien artifact under the ice. YouTube U.F.O. "experts" were feeling pretty smug. "See, I told you so," they said. "They probably built the pyramids too, so, there, in your face!" But the strangest thing was that it wasn't aliens that built the pyramids or the tower. It was us. Just a past civilization that was more advanced than ours that somehow ended. At least, that was suggested by the body found at the base of the tower. It was preserved in the ice, frozen as if they had just died yesterday, although it was clear it had been thousands of years.

They were clearly human, very close to our physiology. Their heads were significantly larger than ours, and their eyes were slightly more prominent, but it was still clearly a human, an ancestor, and not an alien. DNA forensics concluded that we did share 99.9% of genetic material. It was odd that there was only one and no skeletons of others, artifacts, remains of villages, etc. The tower seemed to stand alone, as did its one inhabitant. Maybe more of its kind were inside. Only time would tell.

One of the strangest things about the tower was the writing all around the base of it. The writing was like hieroglyphs, but they 'moved.' At least they appeared to move. They never stayed the same. You would start to read, and then they would change and be different if you looked again. Also, they were not etched or printed onto the tower; they were just below the surface and seemed to have a life of their own. No one saw the same thing twice.

When the hysteria around finding the "Antarctica tower" settled and life went back to normal, a whole school of study grew around this newly found "Atlantis." That was what the Ancient Alien theorists were calling the tower and the lost city it must have been part of once, but Susan hated it. She was sure the city's real name was more elegant and spectacular and had nothing to do with that silly mystical city from that stupid tv show. She wanted to know its real name. She didn't know what it was yet, but as she struggled to decipher its archaic language for her thesis paper, she was sure she would figure it out. He was a scientist. She dealt with facts.

When Susan studied the writing on the tower, she knew it was something unique and powerful - unlike any language she had ever seen. The writing was beautiful. It was the artwork. It fascinated her. It kept her up at night. It kept her intrigued and fascinated and busy, too busy to remember to call her parents often enough or even to think about meeting someone new and going on a date. She was single, and on her way to exploring this mystery was fine by her. She didn't have time for that silliness. She had a puzzle to solve. Fooling around with a boyfriend was just not in the cards. It was a waste of time. Besides, the last one was horrid.

Susan shook her head to get herself out of that revelry. No need to go there now. She's on her way to the site for the first time. Until now, she saw only computer images and videos of the writing. This time she was going to see them for real. After years of obsessing, her dream became a reality after years of study. Thanks to her mentor, he landed her a spot with the United States National Geological Society as its linguist. She could use this amazing opportunity in itself as her Ph.D. thesis project - studying the language on the tower and delivering what it means. Not one to shy away from a challenge, she packed her bag for Antarctica. She would live in the great plains beyond the mountainous area not too far from Concordia. It's a hot mess there right now. Several countries vied for territory; negotiations collapsed in 2067... no war but a few skirmishes. Having a strong Navy played in favor of the Americans, but the Russians and Chinese also have excellent fleets.

Susan was fluent in 12 languages. Call it a gift. She was learning more all the time, even a few dead languages. In this case, a dead one. It would take everything she had to crack the code of the language on the tower. The challenge was exciting but daunting. It would be the accomplishment of a lifetime, and it would probably take a lifetime... she sighed and looked out the window of the jet. Nothing but the ocean as far as the eye could see. The plane's engine droned on and on, lulling her into a meditative state. She dozed.

The wheels hitting the tarmac jolted her awake. She must have been more tired than she thought. The runway outside the airplane was empty. There was no one there to greet her. She walked down the ramp, across the landing strip, and into the terminal. There is no mad rush to Antarctica. It's still hard as hell to get to and not very inviting. The highest temperature to date was 50 degrees Fahrenheit (10 degrees Celsius). And that is the middle of the "summer" when the sun is at its highest. Susan was getting there in late October. She did not expect any Halloween celebrations this far south, but it was her favorite holiday and she would miss handing out candy to all the costumed kids this year. But here in Antarctica, it began a six-month-long streak of uninterrupted daylight. The sun will rise and not set for some time. Susan wasn't looking forward to the sun being up 24 hours a day, low on the horizon. She was less looking forward to the 6-month long night that was behind it. Suicide rates increased in February and grew as the long night wore on.

She didn't have to wait for her luggage, she only had a carry-on and a backpack with her tablet in it. Another talent, traveling light, just the essentials. The only person she knew of who had beaten her in that skill was John, a merchant marine she had dated after undergrad. Susan smiled, remembering the day Jon had moved in with her. She had seen his spartan apartment, but when he arrived carrying a chest, she had asked:

"Do you need any help carrying the rest of your things in?" as she looked for the rest of his bags. None to be found.

John just stood in front of his steamer chest and said

"Nope, I'm done.".

Susan looked at him quizzically.

"Really? Where is all your stuff?" she asked. "Everything I own is in here" John was pointing to the chest. It was a furnished apartment, I actually own very

little.

"Amazing..." Susan said wide-eyed.

"Being a merchant marine for 8 years will do that to you." John's chest swelled just a bit.

"Well then, welcome home!" and she leaped into his arms.

A pleasant memory.

Again she shook herself out of her revelry... two boyfriends in one day, what was going on with her? Has she been single for too long? Never mind, it didn't matter; she had better things to worry about now than being intimate, even though it had been ages.

Her mentor had made sure that she had a vehicle waiting for her which turned out to be an old Toyota F.. cruiser, light blue and still in good condition, with just enough wear to make it look tough. She had gotten the keys from the Avis rental car desk inside. It was an electric convert. The engine ripped out, and ion batteries were installed. The odometer read over 200,000 miles, but it seemed solid.

Touching the screen on the dash, she punched in the address and said thanks to saint Elon and the miracle of Starlink satellite Wi-Fi. She smiled, tired but excited, and hacked into the global system to get directions to the tower site and her new lab. She thought about going to Mars and exploring with SpaceX, but this was way more exciting to her and considerably less dangerous. It still had its risks but being in a frozen desert was better than being in a frozen desert with no oxygen. She still secretly hoped that another ancient civilization was there, but so far, nothing.

The drive from King George Island to the site at the plains was going to be long. The GPS said that it would take twelve hours to get there. The only saving grace was that as the Earth warmed, the ocean calmed down around Cape Horn, allowing faster passage. The bridge from King George to the mainland was a godsend - otherwise, the trip would have been much longer. King George Island had the only working airport that far south. Work on a new road from there to the tip of Chile was still under construction and hotly contested. Chile has always held a claim to Antarctica, stating that their ancestors got there first. Despite the long flight and cold weather, Susan felt ready for a drive. The fact that her vehicle was a modified self-driver said all that needed to be said about this excursion. Very low budget. Which suited her just fine, Susan liked roughing it. Felt more authentic to her, more real.

As she drove, she found herself thinking about the summer she had spent living with a Bedouin family in Egypt before she served in the Israeli secret service during her gap year after college. They were so kind to her. So patient, living in touch with nature, and focused on friends and family. She missed those days, no worries, unlike the madness of her life and today's world.

The desert held a strange allure for her. Maybe that was why she was attracted to Antarctica. Just a different kind of desert. A very, very cold one. Maybe it was the isolation. She loved people, they charged her, but she treasured solitude. It cleansed the soul.

# CHAPTER THREE

SIX HOURS INTO HER DRIVE, she needed rest and saw lights ahead in the fog. The English chap on her navigation said it was a rest stop where she could charge the FJ and her body could be refreshed. She desperately needed a bathroom break and a drink. She pulled in and parked the vehicle in the induction charging bay. Making her way over to the building, it was right out of a western. The wind blows hard here.. she fully expected a tumbleweed to drift by and see two desperados about to have a shootout. "At dawn, we draw". The eternal sunrise of Antarctica suggests a spaghetti western. The place did look seedy, and she liked that; it was raw and real.

Coming in from the blustery wind outside, she entered the saloon. It was a trope. A jukebox in the corner playing some sad country song about a jilted lover with a pickup truck and a gun rack. It was dark, neon-lit, and a wise mustached older man was cleaning a glass with a dirty rag behind the bar. He had deep weathered lines on his face and a worker's hands.

No one seemed to notice her, which seemed odd; she couldn't imagine they got many customers. She sat at the bar and ordered a stiff one, bourbon, Bulliet, rye, neat, and ice water. Jeb, the bartender, turned around and produced the asked-for beverages without a word after a moment. No malice, but no smile either. He just went back to cleaning glasses with his greasy rag.

Susan downed the Bulliet in one gulp and then commenced sipping the water decompressing. She knew her journey was only half over, so she better not have too many. One more wouldn't hurt, and she planned on sipping it. She got Jeb's attention again, and silently he produced the asked-for beverage. This time his look lingered a bit longer. Did she know him? Probably not. Susan was enjoying her solitude. Her thoughts drifted off to what it would be like researching and then cracking this new language, figuring out the puzzle no one else could solve. She enjoyed the attention her accomplishments brought, she admitted it, and this would be a huge victory if she could decipher it. Unlocking stories from these ancient ancestors —what would they say? It would be an amazing Ph.D. thesis. A faint hint of a Nobel prize drifted somewhere in the back of her mind.

Her daydream didn't last. If you thought the female-to-male ratio was bad in Alaska, you haven't seen Antarctica. It's worse, way worse. The men are a pack of hungry, horny wolves, and it's hard for a woman to get alone time. Two drinks in, and not even 15 minutes since she entered the bar, a drunk man slid up to her from the side and slithered his arm around her like a snake. Before he could whisper whatever opening line he would say into her ear, she turned and had him on his knees. The shock in his eyes was immense, and his mouth formed an invisible scream. She had him in a devious kotegaeshi wrist lock. The would-be assailant grabbed his forearm with his other hand, where all the pain was. She heard an audible cocking noise from behind her and knew what it was immediately. A shotgun. She waited for it.

"Let her go, Alex." Said a large man, standing calmly, protected behind a shotgun, pointed at Alex.

"I can't, Jeb!" Alex finally managed to blurt out. His breath was labored and quick.

"She's got me in some kind of fancy karate thingie. Tell her to let *me* go!"

"Alex, I'm gonna ask you real slow like. When the nice lady lets you go, I want you to apologize to her and then go home." Jeb said this in a very low, graveled voice.

Alex just looked at Susan, and her cold stare bore through him. She wasn't easing up.

"Alex? You got *that*?" Jeb's voice raised just a smidgeon on the last word.

The shock was over, and now he was just plumb mad. Jeb could see that. Alex knew Jeb wouldn't kill him, but he *would* shoot him. He'd seen it. Probably in the leg or upper arm, just so as not to end him. Special forces were like that.

"... ok."

Susan saw Alex look at the gun and then into her eyes, and his fire faded. She relaxed her grip. Slowly. Alex stood up, rubbing his wrist, and with hurt puppy dog eyes, grabbed his coat and left in a hurry. Jeb pointed the shotgun to the ceiling and cradled it on his hip.

"Sorry about that, sweetheart. What did you say your name was again?"

"I didn't. And don't call me sweetheart." She downed the second rye in one fell swoop. She placed the glass on the bar with purpose, slowly, never taking her eyes off him.

"Oh... you didn't, did you? Well, my name is Jeb. Pleased to meet you. Where did you learn to move like that? Hassad?"

"Sayeret. I look that Jewish?"

"It's the nose. It's strong but a dead giveaway. That and the amazing black curly hair."

Susan did bear a strong resemblance to Julia Louis-Dreyfus. But better looking, not as angular. Softer. Easier on the eyes. She just looked at Jeb and touched her glass. He immediately filled it for her again. A little bit more than last time she noticed. She took a measured sip, not taking her eyes off Jeb's.

"I was born in Israel. I served in the military. You?" as she put down her glass.

"J.S.O.C.," Jeb said, pouring himself a whiskey.

Susan nodded and took another sip. Jeb was old. But not unhandsome. He carried his age well. He was fit, and that looks good on anyone. He leaned the shotgun against the back of the bar, turned around, and then took another drink of his scotch. Leaning in on one elbow, he said.

"Wanna swap war stories?" He winked. His voice was warm and deep.

Susan smiled. "Not really. I'm tired, and now I am pissed off."

"Ah, relax. Alex is harmless." He said as he straightened up. "He took a gamble that didn't pay off. Most men here haven't seen a woman in a very long time. He wasn't thinking with his brain." He sipped his whiskey, savoring the taste.

Susan remained silent. She took another sip of her drink. Her gaze did not break from Jeb's. It was a cold stare, but there was nothing there. No malice but no love, either. She knew his kind. Old warriors didn't know much about warm fuzzies. Occupational hazard.

"J.S.O.C. huh?" she said finally. "Joint Special Operations Command... party boys."

"Yeah. Stationed at Bragg. Been all over the world. You know... 'making friends'. Helicopter pilot." He had a wistful look in his eye as he finished his second glass.

Susan didn't know what to say. How many kills, she thought, not confirmed either. How many for him, how many for her? So much sin to pay for in the end. Was there a judgment day? Who knew? Nor did she care. She took another sip of her drink and put it down. She stared at Jeb for a long time; he met her gaze unflinchingly.

Finally, he said, "32 confirmed, 50 if you count unconfirmed. You know... 'making friends.'" He didn't smile this time. He looked at her and waited. A few seconds passed between them.

Susan countered. "33 confirmed, 52 un..."

"Well, now, are you just one-upping me here?" His smile broadened from nowhere.

"Whatever you say, old man." Susan winked at him this time.

"I like your style, little Missy. What brings you to the jolly old land of anti-Santa" Jeb was still grinning. He hadn't had a good talk with a fellow soldier in a while, and she was good-looking.

"I'm here for The tower. My name is *Susan,* by the way," she said with a bit of an edge. "You need to drop the pet names there, Captain."

"Roger that, Lieutenant. It's a pleasure to meet you, *Susan*." he mockingly saluted. He paused and was thoughtful for a moment. "The Tower, huh?"

"Yeah, I am good with languages," she said.

"Well, now... that *is* interesting." Jeb put his elbow on the bar and leaned in, but not too close, showing genuine interest.

"How many languages can you speak?" he asked.

"Confirmed or unconfirmed?" Susan looked up at him.

Jeb laughed out loud.

Susan laughed, too, and started to relax. They talked for a good hour. Jeb reminded her of her father in a strange way. Most men were always hitting on her. This one seemed genuinely interested in her, what she did, and her life.

After a spell, Susan sighed; she had a long ride ahead. As much as she would love to talk more with Jeb, she had a mission. She had a feeling for people and could tell Jeb was trustworthy, so she had made a new friend on this continent, which never hurt, given she would be here awhile. She had better get her ass moving.

"I better get going," she said reluctantly.

"I had a feeling I was keeping you from something important. Thanks for letting an old warrior bend your ear." Jeb said, straightening up behind the bar. He grabbed his dirty rag and started cleaning the glass without breaking eye contact with Susan.

"I definitely want to hear more about your adventures as a pilot. You flew some impressive war machines." Susan said with genuine interest.

"Hell, maybe I'll take you for a ride sometime." Jeb smiled.

"I would love that, especially if it was for fun instead of on a mission..." Susan drifted off. "Here is my information, please stay in touch, Jeb." They touched their i-wrist phones together. No personal information was exchanged, only a way to contact the other and communicate if desired. "Just friends" app brought to you by Apple.

"Will do, little missy... I mean Susan. You be careful out there now, ya hear?" He put both hands on the bar and tried to look as fatherly as possible.

Susan let the term of endearment slide; she knew it was coming from a good place. She turned as she was leaving, looking over her shoulder, she gave him a wry smile. She didn't need to say anything. He winked, turned, and continued cleaning the mug in his hand. Jeb knew she was going to be just fine. Susan had a strange feeling that this was not the last time she would see him.

# CHAPTER FOUR

JARED LOOKED at the monitor and sighed. The last of the ice was melting in front of his eyes. Today Antarctica would become a desert land mass. So many wasted years of his life fighting this outcome. How many times had he addressed congress? How many rallies, protests, or hearings? His entire life's work was to prevent this, and to no avail. His work on environmental preservation seemed empty and meaningless, the trope of the scientist that says, 'the sky is falling so much, that no one listens. He met the president and other world dignitaries, pleading his case. "If we don't do something, it will be too late." Conveyed clearly, loudly, over and over again - to no avail. Every single one of them seemed to feign interest. A few tried, but they were swimming upstream.

Gore was the only one to take an interest, and the old man had helped further Jared's career with his support. He even had a minor role in Gore's latest climate change disaster documentary. "Where are All the Emperors?" was the title. The penguins had long gone. Polar bears on the north pole went before them. Some of them interbreed with the grizzlies, but their numbers were thin. "We are living in the next great extinction," he told the uncaring ears of Parliament. Venice was one of the first places to be completely submerged. The mass movement of people to the mountains. Food shortages. Riots. Skirmishes bordering on all-out war, but somehow full-blown war was prevented; the nuclear weapons were never launched n. Jared always thought it was because the silos were flooded. Who knew? Someone did.

What did any of it matter? Life went on regardless. Things changed dramatically, but humans figured it out. The one thing to come out of this mess was the oil protests. He had never seen anything like it. It was the one time that the entire world came together on a common goal. Gorilla warfare was the most unexpected part. Gas stations were targeted as well as offshore oil rigs. Something that had been a small faction of extremists bled over into the general populace. They were done. They wanted solar power, wind... geothermal, whatever it took to eliminate the very thing that was killing the Earth and them.

Not one more penny for the power-hungry oil magnets. They marched on Washington. Jared joined the eco-terrorist, he wanted to change, and he wanted it right then. He was right in the thick of that craze. But the eco-terrorism had worked eventually. Small victories at first, but eventually, gas vehicles were outlawed, and eventually the hybrids, so it was all electric now. Gas was seen as dirty, and all car manufacturers clamored to get their electric vehicles out front of the others. But, it was a slow and painful process.

Jared put his head in his hands. He wanted to weep but couldn't. He was empty. Empty like the gas stations around the world that were rotting or had just become convenience marts. He hated gas; he hated the stations. Every time he passed one now and saw that it was in disrepair and falling apart, he smiled. It was dangerous. Putting an explosive liquid near the rear end of a machine most likely to be hit by another one in that region seemed insane to him. Well, most of humanity *was* mad.

Gasoline smelled terrible. It was toxic. Not to mention how they got it out of the Earth or when they would accidentally spill it, or an offshore oil refinery would catch fire. All ecological disasters. By 2050 all cars were electric, at least the ones rolling off the assembly lines. It took some time for the internal combustion engine to breathe its last. Ironically, as more and more people moved over to electricity, it lengthened the gas supply. The price plummeted. Gasoline-powered cars became the domain of the rich because of the upkeep and unavailability of fuel. They went the way of horses. Owning one became a luxury, not a necessity.

He tried not to think about the bombs he had placed at some of those stations. His time as an eco-terrorist was something he wished he could soon forget - it was the right cause, but the visions of some of the innocents that were harmed in his acts still haunted him. He tried not to think about the man he saw on fire because of his bomb, running away from the gas station.

One of his cohorts recorded it with his Goggle Glasses. It went viral, it was everywhere he looked. He was just the attendant. No one was supposed to be there, but the best-laid plans of mice and men, they say. He tried not to think about all the dry heaving he had done that evening and not being able to eat for at least a week. He tried not to think of how the man's face was melting as he ran towards the camera, his mouth wide open in a silent scream. It was a sin he would carry with him until the day he died. The nightmares had at least been less frequent of late. But they still came. They still haunted him.

The phone rang and startled him. Taking a second to collect himself, he answered. It was the director of his minor department of Mi6.

"Hello, Jared," she said in a monotone.

"Greetings, Carol" he flatlined right back. Neither was thrilled to talk to the other. Ever.

"I need you to get your ass down to Antarctica." she droned.

"Why?" At this point, Jared didn't care for polite pleasantries anymore.

A long pause and a deep breath.

"My superior just got off the phone with some big wig from Washington D.C. in America. There has been a development with the Russians and Chinese, and we need you to investigate. Your cover as a scientist has worked well for us in the past. Some big-shot linguist from Israel is headed down there. You need to cozy up to her." She fell silent, waiting for his reply.

He is a scientist. But also a spy. God and country and the queen and all that. He remembers when he was 'recruited.' The gas station incident led them to him. Being an eco-terrorist seemed like the only recourse to a young grad student studying environmental politics for his Ph.D. and seeing it was almost too late to fix things. The Crown didn't see it that way. He wasn't a double O agent. They gave him the choice of doing their bidding to work off his debt to society or rot in jail. No license to kill. Just an office and having to do whatever they said whenever they said. They did train him in small arms handling. He was a pretty good shot. It did save him on a mission in Prague. Another recurring nightmare. Bond films never show you that when you kill people, they haunt your memories. The look on their faces of shock, disappointment, and rage all in one. It was unforgettable.

"Uh-huh" was all he said to his Mi6 handler, dreading another assignment.

"Go see Nigel. You leave in an hour." she hung up unceremoniously.

Without saying a word, he hung up too. An hour? This was why it was impossible to have any meaningful relationship. Gone, no word, and certainly no explanation of where he was. His last girlfriend, Bethany, wasn't having it. He really liked her, but she had a point.

"Where were you?" she yelled.

"My mother was sick, I had to run," he said weakly and unconvincingly.

"I am not dealing with this. You are a bald-faced liar. I hope that she was good..." she turned on her heel, suitcase in hand.

The door slammed behind her. In a way, Jared felt like he deserved it. It was his punishment for killing that man at the gas station and the man in Prague. It was his own private little hell. Slowly but surely, he was dying inside. It was just easier not to feel anything anymore. It made killing that bastard in Prague a lot easier. Well, maybe just a little easier. He wondered how many people you had to murder before you didn't care anymore. Part of him hoped he never found out. Part of him did. Part of him thought he already knew.

He headed down the hall to the elevator and pressed the button below the basement button. It immediately read his fingerprint and a soft bell tone sounded. A sweet, soft British female voice said, "R & D." He stared at the floor as the box hummed to its destination.

The door hissed open, and a face was in his face immediately.

"JARED!!! How are you, man?" Nigel was happy to see him. At least someone was.

"Meh. I've been better." he shuffled his feet like an awkward teenager.

"Cheer up, brother, you get to get out of this hell hole." Nigel clasped Jared on the shoulder, shaking him a bit.

"Trading one hell hole for another is not cheering me up, Nigel." he looked at his friend balefully.

"Antarctica..." Nigel stared blankly toward the ceiling. "Part of me is a bit jealous. Never been."

"There is probably a very good reason for that..." Jared trailed off.

"Man, you are all gloom and doom today." Nigel tried to feign a concerned look.

"Just give me the details." Jared groaned.

"Fine, fine. Grumpy Gus. Follow me." Nigel turned swiftly and was off.

The room was immense, almost cavernous. It reminded Jared of when the doctor got into his Tardis. It seemed fifth-dimensional. Gadgets were everywhere, with no rhyme or reason to their placement. The sounds of electronics from all directions and a very low bass-toned hum you couldn't quite place but felt in the pit of your stomach permeated the room. Nigel knew where everything was and mostly ignored Jared's jabs at being brilliant but a complete slob of a scientist. They approached the middle of the room, where there was a table with a few items on it.

"Ok, so, here is your sidearm. Sig Sauer p-230 9mm as requested. Dockers clutch. Black finish, very Bond." Nigel handed it over to Jared, butt stock first. It was open and unloaded with the clip out. Nigel then handed Jared the clip.

Jared took it, slammed the clip into place and clicked the automatic slide. The firearm was ready with a loud snap of metal settling into place. He then put on the shoulder holster, slid his jacket back on, and after making sure that the barrel was clear, placed it where it fit snugly under his arm. It felt good there.

*'Happiness is a warm gun... bang, bang, shoot, shoot.'* Lennon's voice

rang out in his head. Great, another Beatles song would live in his head all day.

"Try not to shoot anyone this time, ok?" Nigel tilted his head and tried to look paternal.

Jared looked at him blankly. They balled him out pretty well for that one. Threatened to throw him in jail and call off the whole fiasco. But he *did* complete the mission. The 'bad guy' *did* shoot first. Hell, the paperwork alone was murder, no pun intended. Punishment enough. And that 'Ivan' deserved it.

"I'll try not to. No promises," he mumbled as he adjusted the shoulder strap to make it more comfortable.

Nigel smiled that winning smile of his. His afro was almost comical, it was getting pretty big, and the lab coat didn't fit his tall wired frame as well as it should. The comedy ended there, he was the smartest person Jared knew and one of the few people he still liked. Jared took him in, appreciating his friend, but trying not to show it.

"Here are your plane tickets." Nigel took them out of his lab pocket.

"What, no private jet this time?" Jared said with sarcasm.

It was lost on Nigel. "No, it'll blow your cover. We want you to look like the citizen scientist professor type."

"Well, at least you booked me in coach, thanks for that." a small smile hinted at the edge of Jared's mouth.

"Not a problem, made sense. Professors have a few pennies to rub together, but not first-class pennies. Well, tenured, publishing ones anyway." He turned to a case and pulled out a few more items.

Jared was at least still doing that. Writing grants and being published in his spare time. Science was in his blood. He enjoyed minor celebrity status. Occasionally someone would recognize him in an airport, mall or grocery store that suited him just fine. He was doing small interviews here and there, and Mi6 said that working on grants looked good for his cover. It kept him busy.

"Gadgets? Austin Martin? Smoke bombs? Cloaking devices? Stimpaks?" Jared queried Nigel.

Nigel laughed. "No, 'sole survivor.' You don't have the clearance. Just the standard-issue wrist cell phone with global network access. You know, in case you need to do some research or need to know how to spell anything." He winked and flashed that winning smile again.

"Great." Jared rolled his eyes.

"Take off your shirt and jacket," Nigel demanded.

"What, no dinner first? Not even gonna hold my hand, at least?" Jared said playfully.

"Ok, ok smart ass. You're just not my type, man, you know, being a dude and all. You're not soft and you don't smell very good, either. Now, get that shirt off, I need to stick this into your shoulder." he held up a device.

"We should have done this first, ya know *before* I put the gun on..."

"I didn't tell you to put it on," Nigel responded.

Jared gave him a look and did as he was told. Nigel put some kind of device up to his shoulder.

*POP!*

The pressure was immense, and it knocked him just a bit sideways. Something went in there, *deep.*

"That's how I am going to find you if you get your ass killed. It not only tracks your location but your vitals etc. If you die, we'll probably know before you do."

Jared stared blankly.

"Don't worry, I'll come to get you. Personally." Nigel reassured him.

Jared smiled. Nigel meant it, he knew it. Still, the only person he liked.

"At least this nightmare will be over," Jared grumbled.

"Whatever, Eeyore. Get your soggy bottom to that airport, you've got a mission. Here are your papers, you can read them on the plane. Break a leg, pretty boy."

With that, Jared shook Nigel's hand the way he had taught him to. The first time they shook hands, Nigel said, "Man, what the hell was that? Don't give me that limp dick white boy shit. Here, do it like this." Jared liked it too. It felt real and solid and like it actually meant something. Wasn't the first time he thought about how Nigel's culture had a lot to offer. Nigel even turned him on to a fantastic barber. Said it took him forever to find one in Britain that reminded him of Chicago. Jared liked that it was in a bad part of town, and he was the only white man there. It suited him. He considered him a friend. He loved the music Nigel listened to and the stupid crazy nights they had together drunk downtown...

Jared took a step back to depart. Nigel looked like he had one more thing to say.

"When you get down there, all of the 'other' equipment you will need will already be set up in your shack. And by the way... your contact down there looks pretty cute!" Nigel was grinning from ear to ear.

Jared nodded. "Whatever, man.... I am just not interested." He looked into Nigel's eyes before they parted and wondered if this was the last time he would see him.

"*Whatever, man..*" he mocked, "Just go have some fun for once in your life." Nigel laughed.

Nigel pressed a button, and the door closed between them, and the elevator started its ascent.

Jared sighed alone in the elevator. Would he ever see his friend again? Probably no, not if he could help it. One way or another, he wasn't coming back.

# CHAPTER FIVE

THE DIRECTOR PUT down the phone and rubbed her eyes. They always ached after talking to Jared. Every time. Without looking, she reached for her coffee and took a swig. Cold, as usual. Her chemist husband had given her a hot plate with one of those cute beaker mugs with her name on it. "Best boss ever, Carol." She used it for a while but then kept forgetting to turn it off. This resulted in the coffee evaporating and then burning on the bottom of the cup. Her office would reek. For a while. She did have a corner office with a nice view, but, unfortunately, the windows didn't open. Bulletproof glass. Also, shatterproof, just in case someone decided to toss themselves through them to plummet twenty stories down. Which has happened. Not in her room, mind you.

Jared was a pain in the butt. Her pain in the butt, to be specific. How she ended up with him, she will never know. Mostly she tried to avoid him, let him sit at his desk and rot. It wasn't where he belonged, not according to Carol. His murdering white butt belonged in hell, that's where it belonged. She had dreams of being the first black woman director. She still did. But this assignment made that seem less likely by the second. She kept telling herself that she was "paying her dues," but hadn't she already? Hadn't all black women?

She sighed and looked down at his folder. It was thick. That bastard had been everywhere, and it took them a long time to catch him. He was the leader of the Green Liberation Front. The G.L.F. were well-funded and moved freely around the globe, executing terrorist attacks at will. They still searched for the backer, but they had a pretty good idea who they were, and another department handled that. She was the one on her team that sussed Jared out. It was a blurry image on a security camera at a convenience mart/gas station.

Someone was still in the bathroom, and they came out on fire when the place went up like a roman candle. She lost count of how many times she had to watch that man die. At least the nightmares were coming less frequently. She had a hunch that there was something on the tape that they were missing. It had long been put to rest, filed away, but something about it kept bugging her. She got Nigel to hack the system to get her a copy of the footage so she could examine it more closely. Nigel had a soft spot for her, she knew this. He was like a son to her, and she could feel he appreciated her kindness. She always supported young, intelligent black men, especially nerdy ones.

It was about a month of dissecting the video that it hit her, she wasn't looking deep into the flames enough. She needed facial recognition software to discern a face among the fire. After talking to Nigel, he returned with his results. A figure in the corner could be seen running from the blast. He only appeared after the initial explosion behind the building, so he was invisible to the naked eye. And there the bastard was, running away like a scared rabbit. Only by sheer dumb luck for her he looked back. Only one frame got his full face, but that was all she needed.

She remembers how proud Nigel was when he called her to his lab. She hugged him hard and whopped. Which she never did. She was put together, pants suit and all. No emotion, ever. But with Nigel and this discovery that was sure to earn her a promotion, she let her emotions go for a brief moment. They had got him!

She was allowed to lead the principal investigator to find his location and bring him in. She assembled her team of crack agents, and the hunt was on. It wasn't long before they found him in Prague, living a quiet life with a distant relation. Seems he had put the terrorist life behind him. How he got out of his obligations to that organization, she will never know. Maybe he was laying low, staying out of view until his next assignment. She didn't care. She wanted to bring him in alive. He needed to stand trial for his crime. For murder.

The fact that he was a prominent scientist and minor celebrity initially shocked her. She would come to learn with this job as time passed that nothing would surprise her. It just made him easier to find. It took some searching and fishing around and asking questions, but, in the end, he stuck out like a sore thumb. He blended with the population well enough physically, what gave him away was his need for attention. He just couldn't help himself.

She was able to enlist the Special Air Service to go get him in the dark of night and quietly bring him back to the U.K. She didn't want any publicity. This had to be done quickly and quietly. And it was, to the letter. The quiet professionals, Queen bless them. Every now and then, when he got on her nerves, she would close her eyes and imagine his face when he woke up at precisely 2:10 A.M. to see S.A.S. standing over his bed with night vision goggles and assault rifles. It always brought a slight smile to her face.

But when they brought him in, that was it. Nothing happened to him. He sat in a cell in the basement of some unknown facility for a long time as Mi6 was figuring out what to do with him. This infuriated Carol. She did get her commendation and her promotion for bringing him in, but it was little council when she lost track of him. Imagine her surprise when she got the call from her superior that she was to be his "handler." Her stomach somersaulted. She knew that handling agents was her goal, but this one? It was a hard pill to swallow. But swallow it, she did. She was a professional, after all. Maybe he would get killed in the field, which would end her dealings with him. His just desserts.

Her direct supervisor had called her into his office. This was it, she knew it, her first agent, her first assignment. He laid it out to her as professionally as possible.

"Look, Carol, I get it, it's written all over your face. Trust me, take this assignment. Crush it. If you don't... who knows when another one will come your way?"

She was silent for some time and finally said, "Of course, director."

She put out her hand to take his file. She heard the underlying threat. Take it or else. No more.

She tried not to slam the door behind her as she walked out.

Now she had just gotten off the phone with Jared after getting the call from her superior that she was to put him in action, again. He wasn't a very good agent. Nor was he a double O. Not by any stretch of the imagination. No, he was a cock up. He had killed a pretty important agent of the FSB last outing, reportedly in cold blood, from her sources in Russia. They were not pleased, but Mi6 wouldn't give him up.

The higher-ups did see some need for him, especially on this mission. They wanted him to use his scientific celebrity to connect with some young Jewish linguist in Iceland. Good riddance, she thought. She was ashamed of her thoughts and asked God Almighty for forgiveness.

She secretly hoped that he would not return from this mission.

# CHAPTER SIX

THE FJ CRUISER hummed along the mostly flat empty two-lane highway to Susan's destination. The electric motor didn't make a sound. Most of the road noise came from the knobby off-road tires equipped with the SUV. Most people don't realize that is where the noise from an automobile comes from. The asphalt and the tires. The sky was clear and in an endless twilight as the sun made its extremely slow ascent into the sky for an Antarctica summer. Every now and then, a gust of wind would move the vehicle just a bit to the side, but she had grown used to this.

Soft trip-hop mushroom jazz played in the background on her Pandora account. Her feet were up on the dash, and the seat reclined back as far as it would go. The automatic pilot of the Toyota was working perfectly, so she could relax and get to her happy place. Research and reading. There was no AI driving accident in ten years, let alone death. Still, it took some getting used to. She still tried not to sleep at the wheel. It just felt... irresponsible to her. But here, without passing a single car or life form in over three hours, she relaxed and started rummaging through her laptop for information on the site.

Her hair was in a bun, and a pencil in her teeth. Papers were strewn everywhere. One hand took feverish notes, the other working the mouse as she surfed the interweb. There were thousands of photos of the outside of the tower online, showing writing in the new language. It was the most beautiful 'hieroglyphs' she had ever seen. She couldn't make heads or tails of it, which drove her mad. Ever since she could remember, languages came easy to her. By the time she was twelve, she was already speaking fluent Japanese just from watching anime. The romantic languages came easily to her. She had them all down by the time she left high school.

French, Spanish, Portuguese, and Italian, she felt at home and spoke like a native in all of them. They all felt the same to her, it had always been that way - languages just made sense in her head. They had a cadence. She was baffled that no one saw it but her. It all fell into place in her head. These romantic languages were tier-one languages, after all, and closely related to English. It wasn't until college that she'd learn several "tier two" languages; she learned German, Indonesian and Swahili, loving the puzzle of figuring out new grammar, accents, and speech patterns - a lovely puzzle she could study and master.

Tier three had proven a challenge but nothing heartbreaking; it took more study, but she enjoyed it, and before she was thirty, she also spoke Hebrew, Hindi, Russian, Serbian/Croatian, Thai, and Uzbek. She would study four languages at once. Then she started learning tier five languages: first Arabic, then Chinese, then Korean, and Japanese.

It was as if each tier had its own code when she cracked it mentally, she had it. She immersed herself in each, making sure that she made friends in each language to practice speaking and to spend time in each country to solidify the culture of the language and how it was used in everyday life. She was constantly keeping them 'fresh' as she put it. The ability to converse in so many languages made travel so much easier. Along with her love for languages, she had an insatiable wanderlust.

Was this new language a tier five, or was it more complicated than that? She didn't know of tier-six, would this be her discovery, her gift to the world? A whole new level of difficulty. It was from a significantly advanced past human civilization. She wasn't allowing herself to believe it was an alien culture, she didn't believe in E.T.s.

Her whole thesis would be based on decoding it. She did not know if it would have any relation to another language. She knew if there were letters or word symbols or if there were sentence structure. She had not seen where they side to side, up and down, or in groupings. Was it phonetic or based on ideograms? Its syntax could be entirely unique, making it a tier-six language. More complicated than anything we have ever experienced. If she cracked it, she knew it would make her career. She would unlock the key to this language that no one else had been able to crack yet. She smiled, imagining it unfolding in front of her.

She sometimes dreamed of the Tonight Show being interviewed by the host, Marty. He would be mildly flirting with her, and she would be looking spectacular in her skinny black dress and heels as he asked her questions about what the new language sounded like or what these long-lost ancestors wrote down for us to read.

The press, the fame that would come from the discovery. Faculty positions, grants, book deals, prestigious journals... maybe even a Nobel prize! (They don't give Nobel prizes for this kind of thing, but maybe they would make an exception). A girl can dream, can't she? She indulged in the fantasy, but not for too long. She was a scientist and in it for the excitement of the research, the challenge of figuring it out, and the joy of discovery. But she didn't mind the attention discovery brought

The hum of the car, the drinks, and fatigue got the best of her, and besides her best efforts, she faded...

---

"So, tell me more about these crazy ancient humans! What did they look like?" Marty touched her shoulder when he asked, and the gleam in his eyes was less "scientific interest" and more "meet me in the dressing room after the show."

Tempting to explore the unspoken spark, it would be a release.

"Well, Marty, we don't know anything about them yet." returning his intense gaze. She lightly touched his hand. He touched hers back with fingers that seemed longer somehow. Chills ran up and down her spine.

Without missing a beat, nor flustered like Susan, he said: "Did they have large heads and giant eyes?"

"Yes Marty, it seems that they did. At least from the specimen that was found at the base of the tower. That is assuming it came from the tower or the civilization that constructed it."

"Fascinating!" Marty said, looking at the audience.

"I thought so, too," Susan added. "Their language also looks beautiful." Her excitement about being on Late Night was palpable.

"I know, it's said that it *moves...*" Marty said.

As Susan looked at him, Marty seemed to be changing. She started to see what was off, and his head seemed slightly larger than it had been a few moments ago. Weird.

Susan tried not to stare. She looked out at the audience. She couldn't see anything because of the brightness of the stage lights. She knew they were there, she could feel them. She could hear their laughter and movement.

Gathering her wits, she replied, "Well, the writing on the tower appears to move. Seems that no one sees the same thing. Everyone looking at it sees something different. We have been photographing as much as we can. No two symbols have been the same. Hence the difficulty we are having translating it."

Marty tapped his question card on his desk and looked at Susan intently. "Well, now, that's something, isn't it?"

"Yes, it is..." she answered, feeling slightly uncomfortable. She wasn't as turned on anymore, she was starting to get a creepy vibe from him. Where did his shirt go?

"So tell us, Susan, were they aliens?" Marty was standing now. He seemed to be turning a shade of gray.

"Were they.... GRAY?!" He yelled.

The audience erupted in laughter.

As he said this, his eyes were getting wider and wider and darker, she could see herself in them. Susan didn't know what to say. She couldn't talk at all. It seemed like her lips were sealed. As she stared in horror, his head began to swell. His skin was changing color. Before she knew it, he was on top of his desk, his clothes were gone. He had shrunk to about 3 feet tall and was completely naked. He had no genitalia. His mouth was extremely small. An intelligible language was coming from it. It hurt her every sensibility to hear it.

Susan sat frozen on the stage watching the 3-foot gray no-longer-Marty and feeling at a loss, something she rarely felt and didn't like. The most beautiful melodic music she had ever heard in her head began to play. It somehow soothed her and terrified her all at the same time. He hopped off the desk and approached her. She recoiled in horror. Every cell in her body screamed for it to get away. Marty had transformed into a monstrosity.

He moved toward her ever so slowly and reached to touch her with a very long, slender finger. Her chair leaned backward, and she flipped out of it backward. She sprawled, and Marty started to make a terrible noise that didn't sound like a language anymore. His mouth moved but was not in sync with the guttural noise. He was upon her, almost touching her forehead with his finger. She could feel the electricity between each of them.

He touched her forehead. It was white-hot. Visions of eternity burst into her head, and she was overwhelmed by all the information. From the bowels of her being, a scream started and needed to be released, or she thought she would literally explode. It finally came, and it was the deepest scream of her life. She woke up still screaming and thrashing. She was parked at the site, and several men were outside her car. One ripped open the door. He was huge.

"HEY, YOU OK LADY?!" The look of concern was deep in the furrows of his brow. His thick red beard bristled.

"Wha...? Where am I?" Susan managed to pant out. Her hands were white-knuckled on the steering wheel.

"You're at 'The Tower' site gate. Are you *sure* that you are ok?" He asked again, looking more concerned than before.

"Yeah... yes. Bad dream, that's all."

"Oh, ok. I've done that in my car before. The vibrations lull you like a baby. Hard to resist. What were you dreaming about? Must have been some nightmare."

What was she dreaming about? What in the hell was that?

After a long pause, she responded, "Nothing... I was... just falling. Yeah, that's it, falling. You know?"

"Jesus, you must have been falling from the moon. We heard you all the way from the other side of the parking lot. We came running over. We thought you were being murdered or sumtin!"

"No, no... no murdering here today. Hah hah. I'm ok, honest. Just a bad dream, nothing more."

Susan sheepishly looked forward out of the windshield, hands still gripping the steering wheel. She was unconsciously twisting her hands on it. She wasn't sure if she was trying to convince him or herself.

"Well, that's good," Charles said, looking at her expectantly.

She put her head on the steering wheel between her hands. She had a feeling it was going to be a long day.

# CHAPTER SEVEN

DIMITRI TOOK a long hard drag of his Marlboro red. He loved smoking, he loved everything about it. The nicotine buzz, the flipping of the lighter, the fire, the pull, and then exhaling the smoke out of his nose. He had gotten pretty good at smoke rings too... he always had a pack and the discipline to keep his smoking to four cigarettes a day. This was his evening smoke, and he looked forward to it as much as his morning one with his cup of Joe. He liked calling his coffee that. It was so American. He loved everything about America. The music, the clothes, the movies... the broads. They came in so many different flavors and colors there. Unlike Russia, where the women were boring, predictable, and bland. To Dimitri, the Americans were cowboys, still to this day.

They had pickup trucks with gun racks, rifles, dogs, horses, fast cars, and boots and cowboy hats. They ate red meat like it was going out of style. The giant hamburgers he loved best. Their movies were always about one lone hero standing against tremendous odds. He had always dreamed of living in Texas and owning a ranch. He dreamed about marrying some short stout filly with flaming red hair named Betsy, having a litter of kids on the farm, and raising bucking broncos.

A tablet glowed in his other hand. This hand was shaking. As he stood on the deck of the penthouse of his current apartment, he took another long drag and held it for a few seconds as he mused about his next mission. He finally exhaled, and he thought about what he hated. He hated English men. He hated everything about them, how pompous they were, how they thought they were better than everyone on this side of the Atlantic, hell, the world for that matter. As a matter of fact, to hell with the whole island and everyone on it. He hated Britain, all the islands. His hands grew a little hotter, and they tingled as he looked out over the lights of Moscow. The city's noises and smells reached him on the top floor.

What he hated most, more than anything in the world, was that Brit that murdered his friend in Prague. From deep within his soul, the flame was burning. It was white-hot coal of hatred. He knew his name, Jared, he knew his face. He knew everything there was to know about Jared Thomas Cuthbert the 3rd. Chert! He even had a pompous British name.

Jared had killed his friend in cold blood. Unprovoked. Unarmed. He remembered watching as the bastard put a bullet through Markoff. He watched as his friend stood there in disbelief as he looked down at the hole in his chest. Dimitri still regrets not firing back fast enough, of the shock of watching his friend, colleague, partner, and his sometimes *lover* die in front of him. There wasn't a goddamn thing he could do about it. When he finally had his wits about him, Jared was gone. Torn between chasing the assailant down or comforting his friend in his final moments, he chose the latter.

He cursed as a tear snuck out of his left eye. In defiance, he took another drag of his Marlboro and a sip of his Bourbon, another American habit of his. Bulleit Rye was his current favorite. This time, he swallowed the smoke with his drink, holding it as long as Markoff's dying breath lingered in his memory. It started to sting, but he held it for as long as he could, the pain fueled the hate. It's not like in the movies, his friend had no dying request, no final goodbye. He just shook in Dimitri's arms, his legs flailed a little bit as they tried to gain purchase in his own blood, and he grabbed Dimitri's arm. No one tells you it's pretty hard to breathe when there is a sizable hole in your chest when your heart has been blown out.

It seemed like neither of them would breathe again. Finally, Dimitri took in a breath as Markoff let his out. Dimitri watched and said nothing. Markoff looked into his eyes, and then he wasn't there anymore. Dimitri didn't cry. He just held him for a few minutes, numb. The rage, the anger, the hatred, that didn't come till later either. And did it come? He fed it. He fueled it every chance he got. Like now, when he finally let his breath out, he could feel the blood pumping in his fingertips. He made a beautiful smoke ring and softly said his friend and lover's name. It wafted out over the drop from his balcony like a halo.

"Marko..."

The dispatch came through earlier tonight. He had just gotten it after his late dinner with the escort at Turandot, one of the most expensive restaurants in Russia. The meal cost more than she did, but that never bothered him. He had a taste for the very best. He was entitled to it, it matched his rugged Cosak good looks. He had had his way with her in his penthouse suite and had sent her home. He may have been just a little too rough tonight. She might have been just a little too into it. He paid her, she kissed his cheek, and he knew there would be another session. He smiled. Dimitri didn't care what sex you were, as long as you were good-looking and interesting. He never understood people's hangup with that, cutting themselves off from literally ½ of the world's population simply due to plumbing.

Earlier, he had strode over to his safe on his long elegant legs, squatted down, and waited for it to read his vitals and retina. When it clicked open, he grabbed his tablet. Walking out to the porch, he snapped open his lighter with one hand and deftly lit a Marlboro.

PRIORITY: *Antarctica.*

He touched the screen, and the file opened. The Brits were onto something big, and he needed to be there to intercept a certain piece of intel. He scrolled through, the screen lighting up the scar on his left cheek. Russia had to have it first, at all costs. He looked at the screen and marveled at the tower that the melting ice had revealed. The architecture was elegant, smooth, and seamless. It was positively organic, like it had been alive. The writing was like nothing he had ever seen. It was beautiful, but something was not quite right about it. It gave him the creeps, and he didn't know why. A chill ran down his spine. He continued to read. What stopped him dead in his tracks was the name of the scientist.

Jared Thomas Cuthbert the 3rd.

His mission was simple. Get the alien technology and eradicate with extreme prejudice by any means possible, the British agent Jared. The Mi6 professor. He was also to 'befriend' the linguist Ph.D. candidate Susan. She was the key to unlocking the puzzle of entry to the tower. Discretion was key. It needed to look like an accident. Special note that collateral damage was inconsequential. This meant that Susan was disposable, and anyone associated with her was.

Dimitri couldn't breathe. Finally, after all these years, he would have his chance at revenge. He wouldn't make it quick, either. As he took the last long drag of his cigarette, he thought of how the pain in Jared's eyes would bring him much pleasure. He flicked the butt over the railing of the deck, and the burning ash made an ark in the night sky. He laid the tablet down next to his Bourbon. He pulled his blade out of his back sheath and touched the edge. It felt cold and sharp and smooth. The entire blade was pitch black and cold. It felt *good*. He licked it slowly with his tongue and thought that the next blood to stain it would be Jared's. He sheathed it ever so slowly, knowing that the next time he pulled it, he would be sheaving it into Jared's stomach. He would gut him like a fish, choke him with his own intestines... and stare him directly in the eyes the entire time. He would whisper Marko's name into Jared's dying face.

To hell with being discreet.

# CHAPTER EIGHT

CHARLES WAS A MOUNTAIN OF A MAN. His coveralls barely fit him. Muscles bulged everywhere. He had the look of a man that did heavy hard labor all day and then went to the gym to lift the heaviest weights there, repeatedly. The veins in his forearms stood out like the roots of a gnarled old pine in Yellowstone. He had bright blue eyes that literally sparkled in the rising Antarctic summer sun. His voice was deep and gruff. His beard was thick, not too long, and deep red. He was covered in the tribal tattoos of his people. His head was clean-shaven. Susan had never seen a man like this before. Something primal stirred deep inside her. He oozed testosterone. It came out of every pore.

"Are you sure you are alright, Ms. Ackerman?"

"What? Huh... how do you know my name?"

Susan was still trying to clear her head from that dream, her vision was still foggy. She didn't know where she was. The rising sun cast an eerie red glow over everything. Was she still dreaming? Was she on Mars? Where was the mess hall? She was suddenly famished.

"Oh! Sorry, my name is Charles, I am your point of contact for the site here. The proximity detector let us know you were on your way.

We've been waiting for you. You gave us quite the start there!" His brow was furrowed, and he looked very concerned.

Charles held out his hand for her to shake it. His fingers were so large it was like grabbing a bunch of bananas. His grip was firm but not crushing. Her small hand was lost in the expanse of his. She shook it back, trying to regain her wits. Charles looked at her as she continued to shake his hand absently. He placed his other large paw on her left shoulder. This seemed to snap her out of her stupor.

"... hello Charles. It's a pleasure to meet you." Susan said absent-mindedly.

"Same here. The boys have been chafing at the bit to meet you. Not many women folk in these parts."

Charles saw the flash of wariness in Susan's eyes.

"Don't worry, they are harmless, a bunch of pussy cats. Besides, they would have to answer me. No, that didn't come out right, they are excited to see if you can decipher this stuff. Your mentor tells us that you have a real gift." His bright blue eyes flashed.

"We'll see..." Susan had doubts that anyone could solve this puzzle.

"That we will. Let's get you squared away. Follow me, we need to get you settled into your new office." Charles turned and started walking towards his Humvee.

Behind him, Susan could see part of the tower looming in the distance. It was slick. Curved. Milky white. It was unlike anything she had ever seen. The pictures did not do it justice. The tower was over 4,000 feet tall, almost twice the size of the tallest building built by humans to date. The top was the first to be spotted by the radar, of course. As the ice melted, the vast tower revealed itself slowly over time. Estimates of its age ranged anywhere from one thousand years to millions of years. There was just no way to tell. According to NASA, the ice started to build up approximately 45 million years ago. So, the tower was at least that old. Susan thought older because it certainly took time to build it, how long, who knew?

Scientists were just not ready to say or accept that. It seemed impossible. Just how long have humans been on this planet anyway? Eons, it seemed. Caught in the eternal cycle of the rise and fall of civilizations.

No one era ever wants to admit that its civilization has a time limit, for whatever reason. Or that it is not the pinnacle of human endeavor. Shifts in climate, disease, plague, famine, flooding or any other number of biblical events have a way of changing things. Sometimes it was even a meteorite. A very large one. Susan always suspected that humans had been here longer than archaeologists would admit. We are smart. We figure things out pretty quickly. The tower did not surprise her.

Susan followed Charles to his electric Humvee. It was large like he was. Of course, the man probably had a hard time finding clothes to fit him and vehicles. He picked her up and put her in the passenger seat before she could protest. In one swift motion, she was in the SUV. He was as gentle as he was strong. Before she could admonish him for his liberty of touching her, he had already slammed the door and was opening his and piling in. Granted, she was only 5 feet tall, but could have managed to climb up the side to get in. Without acknowledging her, he pressed one foot on the brake and used his thumb to press the start button. The only indication that the vehicle was running was the dash lighting up with all of its dials and the radio blasting the band Pantera as loud as the speakers could manage.

"...STEP ASIDE WE'RE THE COWBOYS FROM HELLLLLL-LLLLLLL!!!"

Phil bellowed into the mic.

Vinnie Paul's double bass drums shook the Earth.

Rex's bass moved the Hum V a bit sideways. Dimebag's guitar screamed.

"WHAO... who was listening to it that loud?" Charles said as he reached over to turn down the volume.

"That's a classic that will never go out of style," Susan said.

"You *like* Pantera?" Chuck said in disbelief.

"My father raised me on old-school metal. I would fall asleep to Metallica. Human from S&M was my favorite. I made him put it on repeat... It was an hour's drive back to my mom's house. He was in his glory. I used to say, 'Play the louder one, daddy,' and he would put on `Give Me Fuel, Give Me Fire." Great memories for me. she said with a faraway look in her eye.

"We are going to get along just fine," Charles said as he turned his attention to the road ahead. He had a huge grin. He gave her a quick wink as he slammed the V into drive and stomped on the accelerator. Four wheels spitting gravel, they headed east to the tower and her new research facility. Pantera blared over the stereo.

# CHAPTER NINE

THEY DROVE along in silence for a spell, just enjoying the music. Susan's mind was still racing over the crazy dream she had just had. What in the hell did it mean? Late-night talk show celebrities turning into Gray aliens? Craziness. Was it linked to her work here? Was she just tired and obsessing over nothing? Maybe she was driving herself insane. Who knew?

Charles turned down the music via the steering wheel. "So, tell me a little bit about yourself, Ms. Ackerman." Charles' voice boomed above the low music.

Susan nearly jumped out of the vehicle. She stood up and hit her head on the top of the car.

Charles roared a deep belly laugh. "Well, now, if you had put your seatbelt on, that wouldn't have happened."

"It's a self-driving vehicle, they have excellent safety records, so a seatbelt isn't needed. ." she grumbled, frowning.

"Whoa there, I didn't mean any harm. Just trying to be polite." Charles looked genuinely hurt.

"Sorry... I am in a bit of a mood. Didn't mean it either. Start over?" Susan said sheepishly.

"Sure, I am all about new beginnings and second chances. So, where are you from?" Charles recovered his mood.

"Israel, south bank. Near the Gaza strip," she said matter of factly.

Charles whistled. "Rough part of town. That place never seems to heal. Constantly fighting."

"It will never heal. The wounds are too deep." Susan looked out the window, trying not to remember hers. The friends she had lost, the family. The people she had killed.

"What about you, Charles? Where are you from?" Susan asked.

"Samoa, it's a little island in the south pacific," Charles said proudly, his chest swelling just a bit.

"I've heard of it. It would explain the tribal tattoos," Susan winced, she said it with a little too much disgust, she didn't like tattoos. She tried to recover, "It doesn't explain the red beard, though." Charles didn't seem to notice or care, he continued.

"HAH! That's my momma, she was Scottish." he grinned broadly and continued. "She had flaming red hair. She was studying abroad, exploring native cultures. My pops took one look at her and fell madly in love. She passed the male pattern baldness gene from her dad to me, hence the shaved look."

"Somehow I ended up playing rugby for the All Blacks and got hurt pretty badly. Blew out both of my knees. I got new ones, but regulations bar anyone with enhancements. Turns out I can run a bit faster than everyone else. The doc said it has to do with the tendons they replaced and the way my knees don't really have any friction in them at all... I don't understand any of it, but not only can I run faster, but I can jump just a little higher and fall from a good bit of height without getting hurt." Charles said with a bit of pride.

"I have heard of Augs before but haven't met one yet," Susan said, sounding a little more interested than she wanted. "Strange how you have to lose parts of your body to become better than you were and then lose something you love in the process."

There was a long pause. "Banned, that's rough. And I understand that people can be pretty judgmental about it too. I am surprised that you shared that with me."

"Ah... the hell with that crap, I don't care if they know or not. I am still me, just my legs are cyborgs." Charles said through gritted teeth. Seems that Susan hit a trigger there.

"I can't imagine that anyone really gives you much of a hard time about anything. You have got to be the biggest man I have ever seen." Susan said with a bit of awe in her voice.

"You'd be surprised. Get enough alcohol in anyone and they will start something with you." Charles mused.

"Huh..." Susan trailed off in thought about what it must be like to watch this mountain of a man fight. Her feet started to tingle a little thinking about it. She quickly changed the subject.

She brought herself back to reality. "How much further to the site?"

"Not much longer, see that spire in the distance?" Charles pointed ahead.

"Yes, I can just make it out. Isn't that the tower itself?"

"Affirmative, but the thing is, it is deceptively far away. It is *huge*, like nothing we have ever seen before. We are used to seeing buildings that top 3,000 feet, and they are rare. This bad boy is over a mile high without breaking a sweat. Its base is about a half-mile in diameter, and it slowly tapers all the way to the top. The craziest thing about it is that it is built from a material that we can't identify yet. And it doesn't move. At all. It's built in such a way as to let the wind move around it without affecting it. We still don't know how deep it goes into the bedrock either. And we don't know how to get into it. The tower has no doors or windows. It's as smooth as silk. That's where you come in. We can't read the writing on the wall, so to speak."

"You're hoping I crack the code so you can get inside." Susan queried.

"That's right, Doc," Charles said, grinning to himself.

"Well, I am not a doctor yet, but my entire thesis is on cracking the code to this language. Not sure about getting inside, though." Susan said doubtfully.

"It sure is beautiful, isn't it?" Charles said as a strange look came over him. "Every time I see it, it does something to me... I can't explain it. I get these warm fuzzies and a little lightheaded."

Susan stared at him. His eyes had a faraway look, and she got a little spooked.

"Hey, Chuck! Snap out of it!"

Susan snapped her fingers in his face. Charles blinked and looked at her without really seeing her, eyes a bit unfocused, as if e he had come back from somewhere. He gripped the steering wheel a little too tight but kept the Vee going in a straight line.

"I'm good, just thinking," he said softly.

"Ok..." Susan said, not convinced.

"Do you believe in spirits, Doc?" Chuck said suddenly after an awkward silence between them.

"NO!" she said a little too loudly. She didn't believe in any of that guff, ghosts, aliens, cryptids... nothing. Science ruled, and all that other stuff was just crazy pants.

"Oh, ok..." he said defeatedly.

Chuck shut down, and they drove in silence for some time. Susan felt that there was way more to this man than met the eye. She had a feeling that he was not just some giant skull-crushing rugby meathead that had taken up a job as a site foreman. No, there was more there. It seemed there was more mystical spiritual nonsense she didn't understand. What made people believe in that sorta stuff? After a period of time, Charles broke the silence.

"It's just that I have been having these dreams since I got here..." he said slowly.

"Of Gray aliens?" Susan blurted out.

"Uhhh.... NO. That's an Aitu. An evil spirit. No, mine is about a spirit guide. He comes and sits in my room with me. He doesn't say anything. He just sits with me and then I wake up. It's like he is waiting for something or someone. I dunno." He turned to look at her.

"Weird" Susan meant him more than the dream.

"I know right?!" Charles agreed.

There was another long awkward pause.

"Wanna tell me about the dream you had in the car when you got here? It not only scared the crap out of you but all of us at the stop." Charles was extremely curious.

Susan wasn't sure and thought about it for a long time. What would it hurt to tell him? They still had a ways to go before we got to the complex... and he seemed like an ally. Someone she could trust. A friend. God knows she could use one. She had been closed off for so long. No one was getting in, dare she crack the door a bit for this gentle giant.

Oh, what the hell.

"Do you know that late-night talk show host, Marty?"

# CHAPTER TEN

ANTARCTICA WASN'T ALWAYS a frozen wasteland. It was a beautiful place to live a hundred million years ago. Archaeological digs have confirmed this. It was idyllic. It basked in the warm rays of the sun. It is about twice the size of Australia. Of course, Australia is the complete opposite. Everything there wants to kill you or is trying to kill you or CAN kill you. It harbors the most venomous creatures on Earth. Examples: Blue Ring Octopus, Box Jelly, Taipan, Funnel Web, Irukandji, Red Back Spider, Reef Stonefish... even their honey bees. Additionally, it's mostly desert. England sent its criminals there to die. Also, it catches fire a lot.

Antarctica was nothing like this. The prevailing winds swept its plains, bringing warm rainwater to lush grasslands. The soil was rich, and forgiving. The first humans found hunting plentiful and they thrived. It was surrounded by rich coastlands that provided ample fishing. The Antarticians became excellent sailors. They were also naturalists. They studied the land, learned the seasons, planted crops, and practiced animal husbandry. There was no need for the military as there was no one to fight.

Through agriculture, they discovered observation and astronomy by watching the stars. Science ruled the land but with a balance of the mystery of nature and the universe. They were free from religion because no one had invented it yet. When you died, you went back into the Earth from whence you came. They lived here and now, not awaiting some reward after death. This utopia was enough for them. Curiosity drove them to discover all they could about the natural world and beyond. No one starved. No one was homeless. It was like an Eden, and they had no idea it was. It was the beginning of humanity. They had no idea how they got here. Was it evolution, or was it simply luck? No one knew, and few questioned it.

Time marched on. The tower grew in complexity and height. Science was the prevailing religion of the Antarticans. They explored and lived and died and learned and taught. Their developed language was beautiful and complex. They created art, music, and literature. They lived off the power of the sun. Some would have called it the garden of Eden. Others a utopia. Others would later call it Atlantis...

On one fateful day, it was all gone.

The meteor was huge, a discarded part of the Clovis comet tail. The Earth lumbered through it thousands of times. The subsequent meteor showers were beautiful. We still see these showers to this day. But this particular time, the planet tugged on a big chunk of it, and in the next orbit, it was on a collision course.

Four kilometers wide. It hit with the force of all the nuclear weapons in America's arsenals. Tsunamis, tornados, floods, earthquakes, and volcanoes ran amok. The Earth became uninhabitable. A nuclear winter ensued. That lasted approximately a year... Afterward, greenhouse gases ran amok. The ice age was over. Sea levels rose four hundred feet.

The world was in complete chaos. Life died en masse. Not many humans survived. Weather patterns changed. New deserts formed, and other places flooded. Antarctica was now smack dab at the bottom of the world in frozen isolation. No longer was it a lush savannah but an arid, frozen wasteland. Slowly, over eons, snow fell and the ice built. At its own pace, it started to cover the now-abandoned tower. It accumulated over eons into ice-compacted snow. Before the thaw, it had reached one point two miles in height. It stabilized the global ocean currents. The Earth began to heal.

New weather patterns formed. Things settled in with a different rhythm. Some Antarticans survived and started new colonies and civilizations. Cast about like seeds on the wind landing in different places, they developed new cultures and languages. The sun, diet, and location influenced their evolution over time. The city of Anrarticans and their buried world moved from verbal accounts of the past to legend and finally, myth. It eventually came to be called Atlantis by some that were misinformed as to its location in the middle of the ocean. It was never in the middle of the Atlantic. But still, they talked of the advanced utopia of old and how it was lost in a catastrophic flood. Little did they know. Antarctica remained a mystery, an unreachable place for so long. It was all but forgotten.

Time passed. The world moved on.


Jared was exhausted. Not from the flight but from the woman that had sat beside him. He hated flying, but not for the reasons one might believe. He loved the takeoff, being pressed back against the seat. The heady lurch of the plane lifting off the ground. He loved looking out the window at the tops of clouds, not something you see daily, mind you. He adored the stewardess and dated a few. He loved the uniform and how they jetted about, not always being home and in his business. He liked being a booty call. He didn't care if she had a man in every terminal, as long as she was careful and practiced safe sex, he was good. He even liked the little snacks and the drinks, and even the food. He loved putting on headphones and catching a good movie. Sci-fi was his go-to. The air vents were also a favorite, reaching up and having a cool blast of air. The entire trip was soothing.

It was *people* he hated. It would be a perfect world if he were the only one on the flight. Tall thin stewardesses in tight-fitting skirt suits, black nylons, modest heels, and a cap jauntily tilted to one side with their hair in a neat bun, waiting on his every need. Yes, that would be paradise.

"Another scotch, Mr. Chapman?" the stewardess bending forward so that he could hear her over the din of the engines. Jared would look in her direction and see just the edge of her black lace bra from her strategically unbuttoned shirt. She smiled at him warmly.

"That would be *lovely*, Heather. Thank you." he would smile back as he locked eye contact with her.

But no, as hard as he wished it with closed eyes, it was not to be. Just his nightmare neighbor. The one that could not sit still. The one that elbowed him the entire flight. Every time he dozed, she had a comment. A light tap on the shoulder as soon as he was settled into a movie. Making him remove his headphones again and listen to another story about her granddaughter and her poor choices. Or another complaint about the airline or some imagined slight from the stewardesses. Jared wanted the flight attendant's number, but she avoided all eye contact now that his seatmate had been rude.

People were the worst on flights. The guy behind him had taken off his shoes, put his socked foot between the seat and the plane wall, and literally touched Jared's elbow with it. Jared calmly removed his button from his leather briefcase strap, the one that said Manchester United, and stuck the pin directly into the man's big toe. He let out a yelp but to Jared's surprise, that was it. The foot was withdrawn, never to be seen again. Lesson learned, hopefully. Jared didn't have time for that kind of ignorant bullshit.

Her name was Judith, but she was a 'Karen.' Blonde hair, short cut in the back, long in the front, and red, red lipstick. Probably had botox or a facelift. Her eyebrows were painted way too high. She reeked of money and cheap perfume. Headed to South Africa to meet up with family. She thought the whole Apartied thing was blown out of proportion. So much silliness over nothing, she said. This was the point that he loathed her and held his tongue. He knew her kind, nothing he said would matter. He took comfort in the fact that she was old and would be dead soon. So would the messed up way she looked at life. Take that thinking to the grave with you, lady, Earth wants no part of it, Jared thought.

As she droned on about her useless, impotent husband, Jared thought about the upcoming task at hand. He had reviewed the mission briefing from London to Cairo. Unfortunately, there was a layover there, and that is when they picked up his new seatmate. Now he was mulling over the details in his head. Seems that America, Russia, China, and North Korea all have their underwear in a bunch over the site in Antarctica. There are probably other players, but Jared knew from experience that they were of no consequence. There is speculation that there is an advanced technology to be had in the tower. Possibly a meta weapon of some sort. Just like the superpowers, tell them that they can't have something, put it behind a locked door, and they go nuts and assume it's a W.M.D. Sigh. For all they know, it's the secret recipe to the perfect black-bottom cupcakes.

His superiors wanted it, no matter the stakes. Britain is tired of being a second-rate world power. They lost their footing after WW2 to America. They want it back, and this tech is going to make them a global force once again. When you have the best navy, you make the rules. He wasn't sure why they were sending *him*, though if it was so important. Why not a double O? Probably because he is expendable, Jared thought grimly. Probably because he was a scientist and would see things differently than someone licensed to kill. Maybe because he had already killed twice, he wouldn't have any qualms this time. Perhaps he was chosen for his ease of moving around Antarctica, being a minor celebrity there. Everyone there knew about his research and how he wanted to keep their new home a frozen wasteland. Antarticians had mixed feelings about him at best. His mind raced.

He wasn't sure though what to make of this other scientist, Susan, getting attention at the site. She was good-looking, that was for sure, he had a thing for Jewish women. It was the nose, black curly hair, and dark eyes, but it was something more he couldn't put his finger on. They tended to be smart, really smart. They also had calm self-assurance and strong will. He guessed that came from the Germans trying to eradicate them. Susan also wore glasses, so he would have a hard time not falling for her.

He was a sapiosexual. She had a talent for languages, and that made her interesting. His mission was to gain her trust and help guide her to cracking that crazy alien language. If anyone was going to unlock the code to the door down there, it was her. He planned on not only being by her side when she unlocked the door, but he also planned on getting in and blowing it all to hell. There was a time when betraying someone would have bothered him, but that was long ago when he still cared. It didn't matter anymore.

Nothing matters anymore.

There was a final footnote about her that intrigued him. She was *dangerous*. Military training. Wet works. Combat experience. Dan rank in Aikido. Her list of accomplishments was long. There was also the last little bit in the instructions about how he was to shoot her dead once they got entry to the tower. How does one betray someone that way? In the back or face to face? He wasn't sure, but even in his numbed state, he knew this was an all-time low even for him. She was listed as essential and then expendable. His lack of any feeling about this didn't seem to bother him. It was just a job, and he wasn't in the office anymore under those sickening artificial lights.

He just stared out the window as Judith continued to drone on about her daughter's deadbeat boyfriend and how nasty her daughter's divorce was from that wonderful young doctor she had married after high school.

What happened to his life? He had such high hopes. A wife, children, a cozy English cottage with a white picket fence, and a faithful dog. He hadn't planned on becoming a murderous agent for some uncaring government.

Whatever, it didn't matter. This was the end. What a fitting way to complete his miserable life. Betray a brilliant scientist, then betray the world by giving away a technology that could possibly save the planet. He would have the last laugh. He would show them all.

The plane landed, and he waited his turn to get his luggage from the overhead. He didn't say a word to Judith. She got up and said something under her breath about how people could be rude and stomped away. After the plane was empty, he got his bag and walked by the stewardess he fancied. She smiled at him expectantly, knowing what was to come.

But Jared didn't smile back nor ask for her number. He simply kept going and walked down the gangway. He stood by baggage claim until his suitcase came with his gun. MI6 had ways of making it invisible under x-ray. He then dragged it to the uber waiting station. He had already booked a car while waiting. He got in and told the car he was Jared. The car recognized his voice and came to life. It sped toward the tower. Self-driving cars were a blessing at times like these. Jared thought he might have killed a talkative taxi cab driver right now.

Being here in Antarctica so close to the start of his mission, his thoughts turned to how he was going to betray England. How when the time came, he would destroy the tower and himself with it. He didn't feel that anyone deserved what the tower had to offer. Humans would just muck it up like they always did. Take something wonderful, life-altering, game-changing, and weaponize it. No modern miracle of technology couldn't be twisted into a murdering device. No, humanity didn't deserve it, no matter what it was and he was going to make damn sure of it. He pressed the button on his watch phone, and it began to ring.

"Hello," a man with a thick Middle Eastern accent answered.

"Hey, it's me, Jared. I am here," he said flatly.

Are you sure we are on an encrypted line?" the man said in a deep, menacing voice.

"Positive, stop being such a Nancy. Do you have the vest?" Jared snapped back.

"Yes. It is ready. I'll meet you at the rendezvous point. It turned out nicely. It looks just like a regular suit vest." the man said with pride.

"Good, I'll signal you when I am close." Jared looked at the man on his wrist phone. He looked like he hadn't slept in years.

"That works. Just make sure that you wait until I am far away from the continent when you detonate." his black perching eyes stared at Jared.

"Don't worry about that, it's not like she's going to solve the puzzle tomorrow." Jared thought about the machine and whether or not Susan would agree to let him use it on her.

"Still, Quantum bombs make me nervous, *very* nervous." The dark man rubbed his beard stubble, looking around.

"Don't like the neutrinos being torn from your very soul?" Jared chuckled.

"NO..." His eyes darted back to the screen.

"Huh, that's funny. I'm looking forward to it." Jared said as he touched his watch to end the call.

# CHAPTER ELEVEN

DIMITRI ABSOLUTELY LOVED ANTARCTICA. It was dismal. Suitable for his personality. It was cold. He liked the cold. More fashion choices. Not cold enough to be uncomfortable. No ice. It didn't go below zero degrees Celsius any longer?. It didn't get too warm, either. This meant suit coats. Vests. Long jackets. Boots. *Gloves.* Not those god-awful mittens or thick ski gloves. We are talking black leather. He fancied himself a bit of a vampire, so the continued twilight suited him perfectly. Ancient, cold, horrific, cultured, and deadly. He kept waiting for the sun to set or rise, but time was moving slowly, and the sun just sat on the horizon, refusing to budge. However, the streaks of red in the sky pleased him to no end.

The one thing that he did hate was that there was no culture there. Just run down shacks. A make-shift city was forming around the tower, but it did not offer any luxuries. He couldn't get a decent drink or edible dinner. The supply of women here was abysmal. It was a sausage fest. The women here were not to his liking, nor were the men. He preferred skinny elegance in both sexes. Here the population had to be rugged, thick, and tough. There also seemed to be a culture of no bathing and an aversion to soap. He had to restrain himself from spraying everyone with Le Labo Santal.

He had been here two weeks already. He was observing the Ph.D. student do her work. Mostly she did much sitting and thinking, with some drawing and photography. She carried a digipad with her everywhere. He had noticed that she was addicted to coffee. She drank it all day, constantly sipping on a travel mug that said "Swarthmore College" in faded letters. The most disturbing development was the giant Samoan fellow. He was glued to her side. Not that he couldn't deal with him, it was just... complicated things. In his reports, he took to calling him The Stone. Research indicated that he was not to be trifled with. He didn't have any formal training, but street thugs could prove to be unpredictable, having real-world fighting experience. Dimitri knew that he could handle "The Stone " if he had time to plan. But if that man got a hold of him, he knew the fight would be over.

Dimitri fidgeted. His disguise didn't fit right and was a bit itchy in spots. He wasn't used to wearing one-piece jumpsuits. The inseam did not break at the cuffs on his boots the way he always had his pants tailored. As a matter of fact, they were just a bit too high. It was dark blue and had pockets everywhere. He hated cargo shorts, and this was like wearing a giant one. The black boots fit well enough. His name tag read John Smith. So original. The Federal Counterintelligence Service (formally the KGB) did a pretty good job of forging all documents and ensuring disguises fit accordingly. They got him here quickly enough via private jet. The training he received was impeccable, his American accent was beyond reproach. This time he was using his southern accent. His papers claimed he was from Culpeper, Virginia. He went to Germanna Community College, and earned an AA. Enough to make his appointment as a site inspector work. With this title, he could move freely enough if he avoided anyone in a position of power. He blended in with ease. The trick was to look busy, carry a digipad, act like you owned the place, and have a slight scowl on your face as you looked at workers and equipment and pretended to checkboxes. It tended to keep people away from you, they avoided you, not wanting to draw attention to themselves and get a checkmark next to their name.

He found his back story to be typically American. He was divorced with an ex and two kids back home. He was sending the money to them, alimony and child support. Wife: Thelma. Son: John Jr. 13 Daughter:

Sara. 16. Both played sports. Son, baseball. Daughter, soccer. Thelma worked at Walmart as a cashier, they were high school sweethearts. He had a dog named Max, a German shepherd lab mix. F.C.S. was thorough. He had to be able to make small talk if necessary. Dimitri was good at the job, he enjoyed being a chameleon. It was a matter of pride in how well he played his role. He could even "call home" to make it look like he was checking on the kids to make sure that they were doing their homework and getting to bed on time. His contact, Aleksandra, would even argue with him occasionally. She was a consummate professional.

Dimitri was patiently waiting for the arrival of the Englishman, Jared. He couldn't wait to kill him, slowly and painfully. Where was that bastard? And then he saw him. Walking that stupid Englishman walk he hated. So pompous. So self-assured. Stiff. Dimitri put his head down and looked at his tablet to prevent being recognized. He saw Jared walk over to a corner of the area to look at some interesting glyphs on the side of a wall to the east.

He heard him greet Susan, and looking over his shoulder, he saw Jared try to shake her hand. A little too smarmy for his taste. What a charming chump this man was. All smiles. Dimitri did notice that Susan was not impressed. She seemed almost bored with meeting him. She was extremely distracted and kept looking at her tablet or the wall where the hieroglyphics she was studying were. If Jared was trying to impress? Befriend? charm? Susan, he was bombing, and Dimitri couldn't be more delighted. He had a plan of his own to meet and seduce her on his own terms. Seeing Jared squirm gave him immense pleasure.

Dimitri ducked behind some piping that was against the tower wall. Its smooth surface seemed almost alive, translucent. It didn't move, but it still looked like it was moving. It could drive a man mad looking at these writings that moved but didn't move. Out of the corner of his eye, he could see them change. Every time he looked at a glyph, his stomach did somersaults. The writing was not in any letters he recognized, it was in pictures or glyphs he heard Susan call them. They looked almost like tattoos. And the glyphs were in the wall or material, not written on the surface. It seemed to have a life of its own. Dimitri could swear that the glyphs were changing or morphing but there was no way to tell. They all looked the same to him.

Dimitri turned away in frustration. The hieroglyphs appeared to be scribbles of a child, or if it was by an adult, then it was part of some being with a mental illness or on LSD. He couldn't, no wouldn't look long enough at them to tell. Besides, who cares. As soon as that fancy pants Jew decoded them he would be inside the building, get what mother Russia needed to rule the planet and be on his merry way. Well, of course not before he also murdered Jared in cold glorious blood needed revenge for Marco's murder. Then he would spend the evening having his way with Susan before he killed her – Well, it was part of his mission, so it worked out perfectly and at the moment, the world couldn't look any brighter to him.

He hurried back to his cabin to get ready for the evening. It might prove to be very interesting.

# CHAPTER TWELVE

SUSAN SAW him coming a mile away. She wanted no part of this arrogant Englishman, that eco-friendly green egocentric celebrity. What was he doing here anyway? And why was he approaching her? In the scheme of things, she was really a nobody. Just a Ph.D. candidate that got lucky enough to get a free ride down south.

Oh god, he's smiling, grinning from ear to ear. Now he is putting his hand out. Act busy, and don't make eye contact. Pretend he is *not* here.

"Hello, Susan! My name is Jared, pleased to meet you." he already had his hand out as he approached her.

Susan continued looking at her digipad, taking notes on the glyph in front of her. She could have sworn it moved or changed or something, but upon further inspection, it hadn't. She looked at the picture she had taken on her electronic pad which was *exactly* the same as what was on the wall. Why did she think it would have changed? She shook her head and continued with her research. Jared's hand was still outstretched. He wasn't giving up. She could feel him staring at her, boring holes into her.

Suddenly a shadow formed over Jared. The twilight sun was blocked out. At first, he thought it was a cloud, but it was too dark. Then he heard a very deep, not-so-friendly voice coming from a very large man leaning protectively over him, casting a shadow over Jared.

"Is this guy bothering you, Doc?" Chuck said.

There was a very long uncomfortable silence. Charles looked down at Jared, and Jared's eyes widened. He didn't know Marvel was shooting a hulk movie here. But he wasn't green. Jared was confused and felt very small. The giant man was uncomfortably close, and he could feel his breath. Susan sighed and let her tablet fall to her thighs while it was in her hands. She was feeling defeated. All she wanted to do was work, not pussyfoot around with this wanna-be celebrity scientist.

"Yes, he is actually..." Susan sighed.

And with that, Jared was a foot off the ground in Charles' hands. He had Jared by the biceps.

"Whoa! Put him down, Chuck! He's really not bothering me. I mean, he is, but he isn't." Susan tried to release Chuck's grip fruitlessly, but it was like steel.

Charles was looking Jared straight in the eyes, and Jared did not break his stare. This impressed Charles. He had some steel in him. He had seen this pretty boy on TV plenty of times, ranting and raving about the ice sheet melting and the coming doom of the human race. Rubbing elbows with dignitaries and the like. He liked the old-day scientists like Bill Nye, way better. This guy... Charles wasn't sure about him, especially the rumors that he was an eco-terrorist.

"Ok... whatever you say, Doc." he slowly put Jared down, not losing eye contact.

Jared rubbed his upper arms as if he were cold. He was pretty sure that there were going to be hand-shaped bruises on his biceps later.

"How can I help you?" Susan said, not looking up from her tablet.

"Uhhh...." Jared was completely flustered and off of his game. He had missed his shot at being suave and debonair. Who was this cro-magnon man anyway? He hadn't planned on this development. It was the proverbial super strong big guy, the secret attraction never acted upon friendship movie trope thing, he hated that. The guy would prob-ably end up dying for her too. So stupid. For what? Her undying adula-tion? Sickening.

Susan continued to make notations on glyphs. There were definitely new ones continuing to pop up at different places on the wall in front of her. It was a language, no doubt about it. It didn't follow the word frequency chart. They were more pictographic. She was secretly worried that it was just decoration, like art deco. After a moment of Jared not saying anything, she broke the silence. She only did this so she could get on with her work and get rid of the interloper.

"Interesting conversation. Not." with that, Susan turned her attention back to her digipad and completely ignored Jared.

Charles was still drilling holes into Jared's head. Jared looked back up at him.

"Better talk to me, bub... when she gets like this, there is no talking to her. She goes into some sort of weird state. Hard to snap her out of it." Charles folded his arms in front of him and waited for Jared to respond.

After a few moments, it appeared that Jared had come to some conclusion. He stretched out his hand to Charles.

"Do-over?" He said sheepishly.

"Sure," Charles grumbled reluctantly.

Charles took Jared's hand and squeezed it as hard as he could. He studied Jared for his reaction. Not many could stand up to it. Jared's pupils widened, and Charles thought for a second he felt the man's knees give way. But Jared stayed firm. He dug in and squeezed back, even pushed forward a bit. Charles didn't budge. He hardly felt it though he respected the man a little more now. He stood there smiling, listening to Jared's bones grind.

After what seemed like an eternity to Jared, Charles let out a deep, hearty laugh and clasped Jared on the shoulder. He let go of Jared's arm and threw his other arm around his shoulder.

"You're alright for an internet B celebrity, pretty boy! Let's get you a drink so we all can talk and find out why you are bothering my professor."

"I am not a professor yet..." Susan mumbled under her breath drawing away on her pad.

"Whatever you say Doc!" Jared said as he reached over and with a deft gentleness that didn't match his bulk, slid Susan's tablet out of her hands and put it into the worn leather satchel that was thrown over his shoulder.

Susan pouted. "It's that time already?"

"Yes, Doc, it is. You know you need occasional breaks from work. Remember what happened last time you worked too much?" He said with deep care in his voice.

She did remember. A few days ago, exhausted from a day staring at the glyphs without breaks, she had another one of those Gray alien dreams while she was awake this time. It was terrifying. Especially having it during the day while working. She was exhausted from a full twelve-plus-hour day of research. Screaming in the middle of the tower courtyard was not a good look for a future scientist. Charles swore to her that he would never let it happen again. It comforted her knowing that he cared but never came on to her. It made her love him even more, like a brother. He made her feel safe.

Not that she needed it, but it was nice.

She was staring at Charles, and Jared felt a twinge of jealousy. What a look, he missed a woman looking at him like that. He missed a lot of things.

Susan blinked and shook herself out of her revelry.

"Of course," she said, composing herself. "Let's go get that drink and some food. I am starving!"

"Excellent. Let's head over to 'The Cooler.'"

Susan turned and was off. For having such short stature, that woman could move. Charles still had his arm around Jared. All Jared could think about on the walk was ways of getting rid of Chuck.

Charles knew Jared hated him, and it made him laugh all the way to the pub.

# CHAPTER THIRTEEN

DENISE SAT in the back of the bar. She was nursing a scotch, neat. She was also nursing a grudge. Being only able to see out of one eye pissed her off... and it was one man's fault. North Korea contacted her a few days ago and flew her out on a cargo plane. It was a shitty flight, and she was pretty grumpy about it. She took another sip of her drink and sighed. She was gorgeous, and she knew it. It had served her well over the years. Even the loss of an eye didn't distract from her exquisiteness. The injury made it blue, and being a dark-eyed, dark-skinned exotic woman made her look like she had heterochromia. This lent itself to making her look even more exotic and suited her just fine. Being Portuguese had its advantages. So did being blonde.

She was a spy, but she refused to wear a patch. This wasn't a bloody Bond movie, and she wasn't the villain. This was real life. Her freelance career has taken her all over the world. It afforded her the finer things in life. It also afforded her the ability to get away with literal murder. Killing men made her feel good inside in a way that she didn't understand but relished. She had done it from a distance with a high-powered rifle. She had done it up close and personal with a knife. It didn't matter, it felt the same every time. Warm feelings washed over her, starting from her head down to her toes.

North Korea would pay her handsomely if she got the alleged tech that everyone was after. She had no idea what it was, nor did she care. They said she would know when she saw it. That it would change everything... blah, blah. She didn't pay attention until they mentioned that if she did find it and bring it back, she would never have to work another day of her life. The word billion was used, but her Korean was a bit rusty. Infinitely more interested now, she asked about the competing countries and agents who would also be trying to get the tech. One name stood out among the rest. The one that took half of her sight. She had been looking for payback for years. He was one elusive bastard.

She put her finger in her drink and looked directly at the bartender and sucked the alcohol off of it. He was hot in a rugged kind of way. She hadn't killed in a while, she wondered if anyone would miss him. He returned her stare but was distracted by a drunken patron at the other end yelling for another round.

Some of the interrogations she had done made her feel the same way. Inflicting pain on others brought her joy. North Korea had called her more than once to get information from unwilling participants. Russia and China had her on speed dial, even Iran. She was good at what she did. Very good, and she prided herself on this. As she scanned the crowd of filthy workmen across the bar, she tucked a stray strand of hair back into the neat bun at the back of her head. She wore no jewelry, but her nails were always impeccable. He had to be here, somewhere. Was he at a table by himself? Was he in disguise?

She pursed her full lips. Where was that bastard? Not only had he taken her eye, he had also taken her heart. She still loved him. She adjusted her coveralls to show just the right amount of cleavage. Not too much, but enough for an invitation for attention. Blending in mattered, hence the work clothes, but she didn't want to be completely invisible.

Wherever he was, she would find him. She would slowly put his eye out with her knife as he did hers. She wouldn't have to say a word. He would know who was doing it and why, just like he had done to her so long ago.

"Soon enough... soon enough," she whispered to herself. She would take his eye and get her heart back. Revenge would be hers.

· · ·

She took another sip of her scotch and smiled.

# CHAPTER FOURTEEN

SUSAN'S new entourage rolled into "The Cooler' loud and obnoxiously. Jared had regrouped. During the walkover, he was won over by Chuck. How could he not be? He had that big brother protective charm. He was genuine and laughed a lot. It was a hearty deep laugh too. Susan was the first in and made her way to the bar directly. She was on a mission. She found an empty table in the middle of the room. An impossibility at any time of day here. Not waiting for a second, she sat down and waved the men over, enjoying her good luck with the seating arrangement. She just didn't want to stand at a bar and eat.

Antarctica didn't sleep. Ever. It was either light, dark, or twilight. Constantly. Neither did 'The Cooler.' It was open 24/7/365 and was always full. The patrons did a good job of mixing. Even if there was a language barrier, they mingled. They thought of themselves as Antarticains first, Russian, American or Argentinian last. Language is fluid. Different words from different countries were becoming common. The written language was a mixture of Asian characters, kanji, hiragana, Cyrillic, multiple romantic symbols, and Sanskrit. Antarctica was in full swing and developing its own culture, customs, language, and slang.

The shanty town growing around the tower was a part-lodging, part-party atmosphere. But with none of the tight regulations about water, space, or trash that a well-planned festival would have, this was a more pioneer-unplanned festival and there was no free food. It has developed into different sections for different cultures and countries. The worst part was the religious zealot's district. They spent most of their time prostate towards the tower, chanting - it was eerie. They wore hooded robes and kept to themselves, and prayed quite a bit to the aliens they thought lived within the tower. Some claimed to be in telepathic communication with them. 'The Cooler' was just adjacent to this part of town. Susan avoided the zealot district like the plague, walking the long way around to get to The Cooler to avoid it. There was also a 'French quarter,' 'Little Italy,' 'German Straebe,' 'China town', 'New NY', and 'Bedouin Arabia' among others. Each tries to stake its claim around and to the tower.

No one noticed them walking in, the din was bearable but constant. No one noticed them, that is, except Dimitri. He saw them right away. He had positioned himself not to be easily seen by them entering. The Cooler, but he could see them. Jared, in particular. As fortune would have it, they sat exactly where he hoped they would. Paying the barmaid to keep a particular table free helped tremendously. He took a deep breath, his prey was in sight. He wasn't expecting the flood of emotion upon seeing Jared. He wanted to murder him right there and then. In cold blood. In broad daylight. In front of everyone. He almost did but then remembered the mission, the money, the calm delight of dispatching Jared at his leisure in his own time and in his own way.

Susan was certainly not his type but easy to look at nonetheless. He could make this work. She seemed practical and intelligent but still a woman, and Dimitri knew all the buttons and how to push them. Being tall, dark, and handsome didn't hurt either. He made eye contact with her. She noticed him, that was certain. He returned her gaze for a little too long, and then they each looked away. Over the next hour, their eyes met a few more times, and all the while, he was pretending to work on his digital tablet and sip his bourbon without a care in the world. His legs were crossed, and he was relaxed in his chair. He owned his space. He would see her again, no rush, these things took time.

Jared noticed Susan exchanging glances across the room and was curious as to who had caught her attention. He wasn't prepared for whom he saw. The blood in his veins froze. Dimitri? Here? Of course, he was probably on the same mission. Goddamnit. This wasn't going well at all. He was going to have to report this to control headquarters. They would certainly want to know what Russian agent was put on the case. They probably already knew the bastards. Were they trying to get rid of him? His mind raced. If he got half a chance, maybe Dimitri would be in the tower when Jared activated his suit vest.

"What's your poison partner?" Charles grasped Jared on the shoulder.

Jared was startled but recovered. Uuuhhh... get me one of those seltzer alcohol thingies," he stammered.

"One pansy girly man drink coming up!" Charles laughed.

Chuck went to the bar to get them started with drinks, and Jared gave up on trying to explain why he couldn't drink beer. He couldn't take his eyes off Dimitri. Finally, after what seemed like an eternity, their eyes met. There was absolutely no expression on Dimitris' face. Jared only saw calm death there. He knew on some visceral level that a deadly dance would happen between them and thought, well, when I die, the suit is rigged to blow... but he wasn't sure if it would destroy the tower. He needed to be inside for that. All Jared could do was hope that Dimitri would bide his time for his attack and that it happened *inside* the tower, not outside.

He didn't think he would be lucky enough to get the drop on him as he did with Marco. Marco made a mistake. Dimitri was not there in time. Jared didn't think Dimtri would make another one. He knew he was looking at his death either way.

"Hey, what's going on here!?" Chuck said in his booming voice. "You two look like you've seen a ghost. You ok Susan? Not having another daydream, are you?"

"No... no, I am ok." She said as she took her American Mule from Charles' baseball glove-sized hand. She was having a daydream, but it wasn't one she was sure that Charles would want to hear. Christ, that man at the table was good-looking, and he was checking her out. Her toes began to tingle again. She took a long hard sip of her drink.

"So... Jared, tell us what brings your celebrity self all the way down here to the not-so-frozen wastes?" Chuck bellowed over the din. He almost downed the rather large pint of ale in his hand in one gulp. He finished it in his second gulp. He started on his other one and looked expectantly at Jared.

"My government is hoping that I may be of some assistance in gaining access to the tower," he said matter-of-factly.

Susan came out of her revelry. "WHAT?! Do you think we are going to work together? Forget that, no way! I am on my own, you would only get in the way. You don't know the first thing about languages." She was grinding her teeth.

"Whoa, calm down there doc." Charles put his hand on her wrist tenderly. "Let's hear him out, maybe he can help. Who knows? Right? Besides, I am taking a liking to this guy. He is on our side. Kinda reminds me of Bill Nye, but with a penchant for destruction," Charles winked at Jared. Susan stole a glance over at the tall, dark, and handsome, but the table was empty. She had a bit of a buzz and was feeling bold, she thought she might have gone and had a chat with him. A twinge of disappointment hit her, but not hard. She was hoping for a bit of distraction from all of the stress of the research. Oh well, some other time, no big deal.

Losing her distraction, she turned her attention to the men at the table. "Ok, fine. I'll hear him out." She stared at Jared. "But only because you asked Chuck."

Jared was flustered again. Dimitri had vanished; it seemed like right in front of him and into thin air. One minute he was there, the next, he was gone. The hairs on the back of his neck stood up. He could feel him behind him, ready to strike.

Susan waited. Charles grinned. Jared stumbled. "Well.. i... uh... dunno..."

"This guy is a brilliant conversationalist!" Susan snorted. "Are you just a muppet on television? Does someone have their hand up your but making you talk on YouTube?" She took a sip of her Mule giving Jared a challenging stare. She wasn't sold on this guy and had no idea what Chuck saw in him.

"Nooo..." Jared finally managed to get out.

"Well, then out with it. Why should I give a crap what you and your government want? What government, by the way? I am guessing England by the accent. Isn't that where you are from?" Susan spat. She was getting angry, she was hungry, and the drink was kicking in. She wasn't in the mood for this buffoon.

Jared composed himself and decided it was now or never to play his trump card on her. This was not going well at all.

"Our researchers have reason to believe that the glyphs you have been studying have some type of psychoactive effect on the human mind."

Susan blinked. Charles stopped smiling. Jared held his silence for effect.

"How... how can that be?" Susan stammered. "They... they're just a language - lines and figures that represent words, letters or sounds, nothing more."

"Have you noticed them changing but not changing?" Jared challenged.

"Yes, yes I have..." Susan said after a long pause.

"Well, then, you are sensitive to it. Some people aren't. The more intelligent you are, the more you see." Jared said smugly. He had gotten her attention, at least.

"Well, that would explain why I don't see anything doc!" Charles said. His smile broadened. He thought, 'well, I'll be damned, the doc is not as barking mad as I had feared...'. He sat back and finished his fourth ale in a long draw.

"I have equipment set up in my research facility that will help you access the part of your brain that can decode the writing if our theory is correct. If you want to get inside the tower, I think you are going to need my help. We truly think we can help you crack the code." Jared put his elbows on the table and interlaced his fingers. He waited.

Susan sat back and folded her arms across her chest. She felt like a child that had come up against adult logic with no way out other than to comply. She did *not* trust this guy at all. Something in her gut said that he was off. She just couldn't put her finger on it. Both Jared and Charles watched her, waiting.

"Fine." She said, "I'll look at your machine and see what you gave.

But if for one second I think you are not on the up and up, Chuck is going to throw you off of the tower, capeesh?"

"Capish," Jared said, relieved.

Charles stood up and grabbed Jared's hand. "Welcome to the team, Bill Nye!"

# CHAPTER FIFTEEN

DENISE WATCHED ALL OF IT. She saw Dimitri enter and talk to the barmaid. She saw him tap his wristwatch to hers, probably an undisclosed amount of cryptocurrency. She saw him take his strategic seat. She saw the lovely young Ph.D. student walk in with two men. One was a giant with a red beard and tats, and the other was that annoying YouTube guy, Jack or Jake or whatever his name was. She saw Susan catching Dimitri's eye. She saw Jared looking on with jealousy and was that fear in his eyes as well? She saw 'mountain man' down ales like water with little to no effect. He just got louder, if anything. She saw the heated exchange between the doc and the celebrity. But most importantly, she saw Dimitri leave. She quietly slipped off of her barstool and followed him.

Like a black cat, she stealthily stalked him. She knew he was a good spy and would usually know if someone was following him, but she was better. She knew it in her soul. She watched as he entered his shack, and the lights went on. She waited until the lights went out. She waited until he was asleep. She made her move.

Slowly she pried open the window and slid inside like smooth silk, not making a sound. She crept over to his bed. He was completely asleep, his soft snoring confirmed it. He was naked and on top of the covers. She could see every muscle of his body. Dimitri was truly gifted in so many ways, and this was the gift she appreciated the most. She was stirred inside. Slowly she removed her clothes. This wasn't the plan, but she couldn't help herself. It had been so long since she had been with him, and she missed the way they were together. She was on fire with warmth and desire.

She placed her dagger in between her teeth and made her way over to the bed. Deftly she climbed onto the mattress and straddled him. She took the knife out of her mouth with her right hand. The blade was directly over his left eye.

"I've been waiting for you, lover, " Dimitri whispered into her ear. She felt something cold on her abdomen right where her pancreas was. She knew exactly what it was and what it would do to her if it penetrated.

"You bastard. You took my eye, and now it's your turn to lose yours. Frankly, I don't care if you kill me... at least you'll know what it's like to have no depth perception. It sucks." She hissed.

Dimitri didn't move a muscle. He knew she was as good as her word. He didn't want to lose his eye. He could feel cold steel just above his eye lens. Shame, really, the lovemaking with Denise was fantastic. Rough, passionate... unbridled. She gave as good as she got. He also knew that if she slid the blade into his eye, his career would all but be over. Her motivation to do it was high, she had nothing to lose. Why was she waiting? He would most definitely thrust his stiletto into her pancreas, and it would end her. He had to think quickly.

"How much did the North Koreans offer you?" He whispered.

Denise was silent for a moment. She was in a pickle. She had made a grave mistake of not using her initial leverage when she entered and now was caught between a rock and a hard place. Pun intended. She just wanted revenge, and his eye would serve, but she really didn't want to die for it. He had betrayed her. He deserved this.

"A billion..."

Dimitri was also silent for a few seconds. "N.K.W. or Euros.?"

Denise seemed to deflate, and all the tension left her body. She relaxed her knife hand and it fell on the bed next to Dimitri's head.

"Shit... shit, shit, shit." Denise spat.

"I am so sorry, lover." Dimitri soothed. He slowly placed his blade on his nightstand without looking.

"It's ok. I was just so focused on getting my revenge on you, I was distracted." She whispered into his ear.

"We could work together, I could use you. 30/70?" He whispered back into her ear.

Denise didn't say a word. She kissed him, and he kissed back. After a long passionate kiss, they were silent in the dark. All that could be heard was their breathing. Finally, he broke the silence.

"I am sorry, lover. For everything." Dimitri said in a thick Russian accent. He stroked her hair.

Denise's head rested on his chest. "You still have my heart."

"Remember, I don't have one..." Dimitri replied.

Denise could hear his heartbeat. It was slow, steady, strong, and impartial.

"40/60, and you have a deal." She said.

Dimitri was lighting a cigarette, his evening smoke. Took a long drag and after a long exhale said.

"Deal."

# CHAPTER SIXTEEN

THE OLD MAN sat in the middle of the room. He didn't move. He was in the lotus position. His hands rested on his knees, palms facing up, thumb and forefinger touching. His fingers were extremely long and thin. His large almond-shaped eyes were closed. A soft, throaty ohm was coming from his slightly parted, very small slit of a mouth. He was floating about an inch off of the cushion. His head was slightly larger than an average human and his skin was grayish. He was completely naked and had no genitals. Susan wasn't even sure if it was an old man or not, it just looked male, in a way. Actually, it seemed genderless, maybe it wasn't a person, but it definitely confused her. She didn't know how she got here, nor where she was, for that matter. It was completely black but she could still see the figure in front of her. Somehow the creature was illuminated. No, that's not right, it glowed. That still wasn't right... it had an aura. That was it. It was outlined in blue light. She didn't feel any fear or malice from it. It wasn't like the other dreams she had had, she sensed no aggression or inherent harm toward her.

Only calm peace.

She stood looking at him/her/it for a while. Its large oval eyes remained closed. It had no hair on its body whatsoever. Slowly it began to spin in place. Susan didn't think this was deliberate, just an effect of being in mid-air. It was drifting. The oddest thing is that she was drifting with it. She knew that she was dreaming. She had been practicing lucid dreaming ever since the first nightmare vision. She wanted to be able to deal with whatever was happening to her lucidly. She really got into it in college, and then her interest waned. You could only fly so many times or talk to long-lost relatives over and over. It got old and pointless to her. Now it seemed to have merit. Maybe it could help her unlock what was happening to her.

She didn't know what course of action to take, so she sat down in the lotus position and joined in the meditation. Once she was deep in dream meditation, it opened its eyes and spoke to her.

"You are calm now," it said as it floated toward her. Its hand was outstretched, and it slowly brought its forefinger up and touched her forehead Anja Chakra. Susan felt a wave of nonsexual pleasure pulse through her.

Susan looked into its eyes. Large and completely black. She could see herself in them. It was like looking into a quantum singularity. She felt she was just about to cross the event horizon and be spaghettified.

"Yes, I am fully centered and focused. I haven't felt like this in such a long time." She was floating an inch off of the cushion that somehow seemed to materialize from a small seed on the floor. Vines and branches and leaves were growing every which way. The stars danced around them in the vacuum of space. All of the colors of the spectrum mixed and spun behind them like a tie-dyed shirt.

"You are a troubled soul Susan. We see that. But you are also special. Do you realize that? No one else has ever gotten this far." Its voice was melodic and gender-neutral. It was soft and almost song-like.

"I don't feel special... and I am haunted by the murders I have committed in the name of patriotism for my country and religion." She whispered this, trusting this being and ashamed of her warrior-like past.

"We know that. The 'others' prey upon that fear. They will remind you of it every chance they get. They don't want you to find peace and the clarity to get in." It sang softly.

"In? In where? The Tower? Are we there now?" Susan's voice rose slightly in excitement. Would this help being her crack the code? Would they somehow let her in?

"See... you *are* special and extremely intelligent and *sensitive.*" It spoke reassuringly.

It removed its finger from her forehead and proceeded to float around her. Its voice was a perfect mix of male and female, authority and gentleness. It was like music, it was the only way that Susan could describe it.

"Remember, the past is an illusion. It is a story we tell ourselves over and over again. We think it defines us when it does not. You are a new human every day when you awake, then you 'remember' who you are, your troubles, and your concerns. You are not that person anymore. You don't even have the same atoms in your body, they have all been replaced over time with new ones. Those terrible things you did so long ago were done by another person entirely." It continued to float around her as it spoke. Susan remained still, the being was orbiting her.

Susan pondered this for a moment. It made sense. She had grown so much from those angry days of youth. Could she forgive those that murdered her relatives? Her parents in that bomb? Her brother in cold blood by that Palestinian? She had exacted her revenge, but at what cost to her soul?

"You are not even real. There is no matter, no hard stuff, no particles. Only energy and information, quantum relativity waves. What are atoms really made of? The deeper your science goes, the more they don't understand. Is there really anything at all that deep? Neils Bohr knew this. Einstein did not... spooky to him. He could not unify his theory because of his narrow view of the quantum realm." It was on her left now, moving towards her front.

Slowly it began to simmer and became transparent. At first, Susan was confused, then realized that it was fading from view.

"Wait! I have so many questions! Who are you? What is going on? What did you mean I am not real? Help me!"

The entity just smiled as it was vanishing.

"Let go, Susan... let go." It held up its palm toward her as a symbol of peace.

And it was gone.

# CHAPTER SEVENTEEN

SUSAN WOKE up in a cold sweat. What in the hell was that? Let go? Let go of what? She sat on the edge of her bed and wondered what the hell was going on. She put her head in her hands and breathed out a very long breath. At least it wasn't a waking nightmare like she's been having. At least it wasn't the Grays this time. It was sort of Gray like, but not a monster. More human, less scary. When she encountered the Grays in her visions, every cell in her body screamed to get away from it. It was primal. This was different. She felt at peace and comfortable with this creature.

She was startled by a knock on her door. It was Chuck, on time as usual. She had completely slept through her alarm. She trudged over to the door and opened it. She was exhausted even though she had over a full night's sleep. Plus, she was a little hungover from the previous day's activities. They would have closed the bar if it actually closed.

"Good morning Doc, how ya doing today?" Charles said in a deep, friendly voice.

"Ugh... don't ask. I feel like holy hell." She didn't look at him as she rubbed her temples, trying to relieve the ache.

"Got yourself a bit of a hangover there, doncha doc?" Charles chuckled.

"No, well, yes. It's more than that...". She walked over to her coffee emitter and told it to make her a very strong cup. She took the molecular-generated hot cup from the dispenser and walked to a cabinet. She rummaged through it and finally found a bottle of aspirin. She shuffled over and sat down at her small dining room table. She took a tentative sip after blowing on the coffee for a few minutes.

"Remember when we first met, you told me about some kind of spirit that was bugging you." She said after a few sips and swallowing three pills.

"You mean Fetu?" Charles said, leaning back. He took a sip out of his travel mug.

"Doesn't that mean Star, the god of the night?" Susan queried.

Charles stared at Susan for a minute. "I keep forgetting that you are an amazing linguist! Exactly. You really surprise me sometimes doc, you know that, right?" He put his hand on her hand gently for a brief second.

Susan blushed. She liked compliments, as much as she hated to admit it, and Charles just made her feel all warm and fuzzy. He was such a teddy bear. Just like her brother made her feel at home.

"Thanks. Can you describe Fetu to me? What does it look like in your dreams?" She took another sip of her black coffee; the pills and caffeine were starting to do their job.

"Well... he's always sitting in a lotus position, and he never says anything to me. He's just there. He never opens his eyes, either. He does hum, however. It's this long constant drone." He said pensively, deep in thought.

"Huh, mine did the same thing, but it talked to me." She was starting to feel somewhat human again.

"Really? What did he say?" Charles got excited and leaned in. Susan was talking to a God as far as he was concerned.

"It told me to let go. That I didn't really exist. That my past is an illusion... it was all very confusing." She looked into her coffee and could see her reflection. She seemed pretty real to herself...

"Actually, it makes perfect sense to me. It's part of my culture. I'll explain later after we get breakfast." Chuck was famished.

"What did it look like?" Susan continued.

"He's grayish, the head is slightly larger, along with big almond-shaped eyes. No body hair at all. Really long fingers. Small slit for a mouth. No genitals, but he really looks male to me...." he was staring over at the window, looking out to the tower base.

"Jesus, we are dreaming of the same creature. That's messed up." Susan said softly.

"It is doc... totally. But really fascinating too. You seemed to have tapped into the spirit world." His eyes were wide with wonder, and he spoke in an awed tone.

Immediately Susan reacted. Not one that she liked. She hated all of that mystic mumbo jumbo. It had no place in her world. This conversation was over. Period.

"I need some breakfast," Susan said as she stormed out of the shack.

# CHAPTER EIGHTEEN

"WHAT'S EATING at you doc? I've seen you upset before, but it's like you're mad at me this time. Did I say something wrong back at your shack?" Charles said with genuine concern in his voice.

Susan was silent for a long time. She sipped her coffee and brooded. Her long dark curly hair fell over her face, hiding her eyes from Chuck. She was mad at him, but, for the life of her, she didn't know why. Dreams were just that, dreams, your mind working things out. It was playing out fears or desires. Trying to make sense of the day. At best, it was a playground to work out issues or experiment if you practiced your lucid dreaming. No, this was something different. Ever since her parents had lied to her about Santa and the Easter Bunny and the Tooth Fairy, she wanted to have nothing to do with the occult. Religion was out. It was a foolish lie to her, just as ridiculous as a fat man in a red suit delivering presents to all the world's children in one night.

Now she was dealing with the mystic head-on. It was happening to her. *Her*. This would not do. It wasn't scientific. It was always laughable to her, and she looked down on those that believed it. They were mindless children looking for an answer that only science could provide.

"I am mad, pissed, actually. Kind of at you too. You believe that crap, don't you?" Susan spit out the words with venom.

"Hey now... slow down there, doc. That kinda hurt. My people have a proud culture that goes back way further than any of your western heartless science bullshit. There is some real wisdom there." Chuck looked genuinely hurt. Susan could see it in his eyes through her hair. She took another sip of her coffee. She softened a bit and her shoulders relaxed. Chuck could see this. He continued.

"There is more to life than meets the eye. You're a scientist. And as a scientist, you know about the quantum world. Weird shit happens down there. It's a particle, it's a wave, it's everywhere and nowhere. It's only there when you observe it. It's wacky."

Susan continued to look at him, remaining silent.

"Let me ask you a question. What animates DNA? What gets it to unravel and copy itself? Is it just a chemical reaction? You've seen the Harvard videos back when they first tried to show what it was doing in real-time. It's positively freaky, especially how fast it does it. It just goes on from there. Molecular machines, cells functioning, organs doing their job. Your brain. Where do thoughts come from? Ideas?" He looked at her questioningly. His eyes were soft.

Susan thought about this... was she just a mindless chemical molecular machine that was just trying to survive, shove food through its tube only to replicate and then one day die? Or was there more to all of this? She softened a little more and pulled her hair back into a loose ponytail and looked at Charles, softly this time.

"The point is, doc, what are we, really? And if you go further into atoms, what are they made of? Is there an underlying force? Something more?" His hands were gesturing wildly.

"You mean *God*?" Susan said this with as much disdain as her voice could manage. "Don't give me that bullshit. It's a cop-out, and you know it."

"That's what some people call it. That's cuz it's a mystery doc, no one knows. No one ever will. I think you need to open up to the possibility that there is more to life than just cold hard facts. How do you explain love?" He looked at her deeply.

Susan ignored this. She wasn't sure she knew what it was or if that was even a real thing. Just another stupid chemical reaction. She loved her parents, that was certain. In that way, it was very real to her, but romantic love? Hogwash.

"All I am saying is that we are in uncharted territory here, and we need to work together and stretch our minds and boundaries." He grabbed her hand and squeezed it gently. "We are in this together, doc."

At that moment, as if on cue, Jared walked up to their table, and they both clammed up.

"What, what were you talking about?" Jared said loudly.

"Nothing," they both said together.

"Uh-huh. Whatever you say." Jared shifted on his feet uneasily in the awkward silence. He decided to break it.

"So, Susan, are you ready to try connecting with the device that my government provided for you to translate the alien hieroglyphs?" He looked at her, waiting for a response, unmoving.

"They weren't aliens, *Jared*, they were human." Susan was in no mood for this, this early. "Just because their remains don't look like us, they are almost genetically identical." The hangover still lingered, not quite gone yet.

"Whatever you say… and that's beside the point. What's important is cracking the code of the language so that we, I mean you, can gain entry." He looked around him nervously as if someone might be spying on him or coming up behind him.

Susan didn't know what to make of any of this. All of her efforts to make heads or tails of the ancient cryptic language had failed. She was good at this, why was this language proving so elusive? One thing was for sure, she did not like Jared nor did she want to help him or receive his charity. Not to mention it would benefit his country, and she would have to cite him in her research paper, and that was not what she wanted. She looked at Chuck in despair. Chuck knew her well enough by now to know she was asking for any kind of guidance.

After a long pause, Charles spoke slowly and calmly.

"What have you got to lose, doc? How long have you been working on this with no results? Months?" He said imploringly. He looked at her and waited.

Susan could tell for the first time that maybe Chuck was starting to have doubts that she would be able to crack the language. She knew that she was beginning to worry, but she hadn't expressed them. After a long silence between the three of them, she spoke.

"Ok," was all she said.

# CHAPTER NINETEEN

JARED'S RESEARCH facility was dimly lit. He had insisted on doing it there since the equipment was already set up, and moving it would have been too much work. It was quite the setup. Susan was shocked by how much work it must have taken to set everything up. Chuck whistled.

"Quite the setup you have here, J!" He looked around in wonder at all the dials, lights, and gauges.

Lights blinked, and machines hummed. It was positively a doctor Frankenstein's lab with wires every which way. In the center of the room was a chair with a headpiece. This obviously was supposed to go over the intended subject's head. Susan immediately wanted no part of it. It filled her with a sense of dread that she had never experienced. She froze. Jared moved silently and swiftly through the maze like a spider in a web. Deftly he turned dials and pushed buttons. He was mumbling to himself quietly, not noticing either Charles or Susan.

Jared made his way to the chair, made a few final adjustments, and then turned to Susan.

"Whenever you are ready..." he gestured towards the chair.

Susan did not move.

It looked like an electric chair to her.

"I've changed my mind." She turned to go.

Jared had a brief moment where he considered pulling his gun on her and making her sit her butt down, but then he looked at Charles and changed his mind. He knew that Charles would give his life for Susan. He knew that he would take a bullet for her. He really didn't want to piss this guy off. He knew that if he got a hold of him, he would pull him apart.

This time it was Jared who looked at Charles for help. His eyes implored it.

"You ok, Doc?" Charles said this as she reached the door.

"No, I feel sick. To my stomach. In my very soul." She looked queasy. She stopped at the door and put both hands on her stomach. She felt like she might vomit.

"Ok... Well, take a deep breath, you don't have to do this if you don't want to. We can just bounce. But.... you may never crack this code if you don't. I'll support you either way." Charles looked over to Jared and shrugged.

Susan knew he meant it. This past month with Charles had proved to her that someone on Earth had her best interest at heart and didn't just want to get into her pants. He was a true friend and companion. She did want to do whatever it took to crack the code, but try as she might, she just couldn't get her legs to work to move her towards that chair. She stood there for what seemed like an eternity. Her mind whirled. She felt faint.

"Hey there now, I got you." Charles put his hand on her shoulder to steady her. "Let's go. Decision made."

"No... no... I got this, just... just give me a minute." Her hand was resting on the door, and she was breathing heavily.

"Ok, doc, whatever you say," Chuck said. He was watching her closely.

After a few seconds, Jared spoke up. "It's painless. I have used it before. It will not hurt you. I am *not* going to hurt you. You have my word." He added.

Susan straightened up and looked at Chuck. She patted him on his arm to say it was ok. Slowly she made her way to the chair. It took every ounce of willpower that she had. She had to know. As much as every cell in her body was screaming no, she pushed on. Charles walked with her, his hand on the small over her back for gentle moral support. He helped her into the chair, sat beside her on a stool and held her hand. Susan took great comfort in this; it didn't lessen her fear, but it gave her courage. Jared came up behind her and slowly lowered the apparatus onto her head. He moved around to the front of her and placed sensors on her arms, head, and ankles. He moved back to the controls at the back of the room.

"I am going to help your brain reach Gamma wavelengths. Gamma was dismissed as 'spare brain noise' until researchers discovered it was highly active in states of universal love, altruism, and the higher virtues. Gamma is also above the frequency of neuronal firing. It will modulate perception and consciousness, as it relates to expanded consciousness and spiritual emergence." Jared spoke matter-of-factly as a research scientist would do at a lecture hall.

"So, basically, your government has figured out how to tap into the spiritual world?" Chuck whispered.

"Yes, it has. There will be an initial shock to your system, Susan. You might feel like you are dying. But I assure you that you are not... just focus on your breathing, and it will pass. I have contacted my superiors, and they firmly believe you have some kind of connection here to... whatever lived here. It will be like you are having a waking hallucination." Jared was still busy pressing buttons, turning dials, and punching in code on the light keyboard.

Susan remained silent and braced herself for what was to come. The humming in the shack increased, and the lights blinked faster. Jared was turning a large dial and watching a view screen. Susan closed her eyes and squeezed Chuck's hand as hard as she could.

"You will reach Gamma in 5..."

Her heart was racing.

"4"

Ok, got to go now, we can stop this, let me out of this chair...

"3"

Oh My God, What's Happening To Me
" 2"
I can't breathe.
"1"
My heart has stopped!


Susan finally knew what it felt like to die.

# CHAPTER TWENTY

THE FALLING sensation gave way to the sensation of floating. She was surprised that dying could feel so wonderful, so calming, so freeing. She wasn't breathing; her heart wasn't beating... she had no physical sensations. She just was. She existed. She was aware of everything. She heard Jared and Chuck's hearts beating. She could feel their breathing. She could see their auras, their life forces. She loved everything and everyone all at once. The universe was perfect; it needed no correcting or altering. She knew that she was immortal and timeless. Everything was. She felt compassion and understanding that she had never known or knew existed. For a brief moment, she felt like the Buddha herself. She understood on a visceral level that all creatures have a buddha nature. She wanted to dedicate her life to helping all beings achieve this state of bliss she now knew.

Nirvana.

Slowly, the room began to shimmer and warp and fade. It was slowly being replaced by a figure in the middle. It was floating above a cushion and in the lotus position. She recognized it immediately as the creature that had been coming to her in her dreams.

It opened its large almond eyes, darker than Cygnus X-1, and she could see herself reflected in them.

"Hello, Susan. I see that you finally made it. You are the first one in over a millennium. We have been waiting for you very patiently. Fetu began to despair that anyone would. Fetu has been trapped for so long..." it sang.

"Trapped?" Susan asked.

"Yes... more or less. We are still 'alive' within the tower. My consciousness is contained in the great orb. It is self-contained. We are in what you might call a self-induced exile. It was the only way to ensure that our knowledge didn't fall into the wrong hands or worse..." it trailed off.

"Worse - meaning a threat from those beings, the Grays I have been having nightmares about." Susan offered.

"That is correct. They are an abomination of human evolution. Science runs amok, pushed to its extremes. They have lost their way. They value knowledge above all else. They are devoid of compassion. You are just bugs to them, to be tested and experimented on, genetically manipulated." It said this with great sadness in its voice.

"Jesus, this is like the X-files gone horribly wrong." Susan hissed.

"It's worse. Open your mind, and I will show you what happened so long ago..." Fetu spread its arms and started to hum.

All faded, and she was walking in the city during its heyday. All manners of people populated it of all shades, shapes, sizes, and colors. They all had large heads; she could not tell if they were male or female. She could see the distant Tower shining brightly in the noonday sun. As she walked among its inhabitants, she could hear the creature talking to her. "You see, Susan, we evolved into a neutral genderless race. We had discovered how to replicate ourselves without sex. Sex is a huge distraction in the pursuit of the higher self. Without having to be born vaginally, there was no limit to the size our brains could reach. We used genetics to rid our future offspring of the need for genitals. Our world truly became a utopia. Machines did all our work for us, and our energies were spent pursuing knowledge. How to live in accordance with nature. Form a balance. We truly became explorers." Fetu was humming this gently.

"What went wrong?" Susan asked.

"The Others. They were a faction of scientists who wanted to push the limits of the human mind. They continued the genetic manipulation of the size of their brains. They cloned themselves when it suited them, or one died in an unforeseen accident. Accidents were rare, but the universe is a dangerous place. They became immortal. To them, the body became a trap, a nuisance to be minimized. It was a distraction. It had needs. Food, rest, sleep... so they minimized it, hence their small stature. They don't eat; they consume a liquid that provides all they need. Taste was also a distraction; mouths were a necessary evil." Fetu looked at her. There was no expression on its face.

Susan pondered this as she walked towards the main Tower in her dream state. She passed a few of the creatures that were mentioned. They were small and in a hurry to be anywhere other than where they were. The inhabitants avoided them and gave them a wide berth.

"They left us here on Earth to live on the dark side of the moon and beyond. We had nothing to offer them until they started to abduct us for experiments." It said.

"Experiments?" Susan asked incredulously.

"We had our suspicions but no proof. Individuals would suddenly vanish without a trace. It was the y explanation until an abductee escaped and returned to tell the tale." Fetu still had no expression, but Susan could hear the sadness in its voice.

"And then the world tilted on its axis, and everything changed. I was the last soul left alive here and in charge who trained my whole life for that moment and this one." It reached out and took Susan's hand.

"And that's where I come in? How in the world can I help you? I am just a normal human." Susan held Fetu's hand back. Its long fingers wrapped around hers.

"That is enough for now... just know that now that you have unlocked your brain, you can read our writing now," Fetu said, squeezing her hand gently.

"How?" Susan stammered.

"You will know..." it said.

And with that, the city around her began to fade. The world swayed and moved. She felt like she was on the deck of a ship in the middle of the ocean during a violent storm.

"Wait!" Susan screamed as she felt her heart start up again. She took a large gasp and was hyperventilating. She sat up, ripped the helmet off her head, and fell forward, sprawling onto the floor. Charles was so shocked that he didn't have time to react. He still had a hold of her hand, which twisted her in an awkward way as she fell. Jared watched it all play out.

"Welcome back, Susan," he said calmly.

Susan just panted breathlessly on her hands and knees.

"How was your trip?" he quietly asked her.

She didn't answer. Charles was still holding her hand and helping her to her feet. He looked her in the eyes, studying her.

He asked, "You ok?"

"Yes, I think so, just give me a minute."

"You scared the bejesus out of me." He eased her back into the chair. "What did you see? What happened? You looked so peaceful."

Susan was quiet for a few minutes. She looked at Charles and then at Jared. She focused all of her attention on them.

Slowly, she spoke.

"I can read the hieroglyphs now..."

# CHAPTER TWENTY-ONE

THE SEXUAL PLAY CONTINUED UNABATED, and Denise was content. As she lay there with her head on Dimitri's chest, scratching lightly and cooing, she thought she didn't care if they got into the tower. She came to even the score with Dimitri, which turned out completely different than she had expected. But she knew better. She knew Dimitri would see the mission through to its bitter end, regardless of the consequences. She also knew there was no way of talking him out of it. She could see him brooding, thinking, scheming. He was always quiet but even more so these past few days. She could totally blow the North Koreans off. But the Russians... Dimitri was trapped. She wasn't sure that was entirely true; he loved mother Russia. His blood ran red with the flag; his blood cells were probably shaped like hammers and sickles.

Dimitri was smoking his evening cigarette in bed. Smoke was always best after a session with Denise. She was a good lover and bedmate. She gave as good as she got. He could feel her sigh on his chest, but he ignored it. He had imagined that she was having thoughts of a cottage and children or some other silly female fantasy. That was her problem; she had *feelings*. That was a liability in this line of work. No, she was simply a distraction while he waited to make his next move. Seducing the doctor.

Denise mused about marrying Dimitri and having gorgeous children. Living somewhere in Switzerland among the mountains, away from all of the madness. Learning to speak another language, adopting another culture, sending the kids off to school, and having dinner waiting for Dimitri when he got home from his teaching job. Making love deep into the night after the children were put to bed. After Dimitri read them a bedtime story of course.

Abruptly Dimitri spoke.

"I must seduce the Susan woman."

Denise snapped back to reality.

"What did you say...?'

"I must seduce Dr. Ackerman. You must help me; it is the only way that I will gain access when she cracks the code." Dimitri took a long drag of his American Marlboro Red 100.

"Must you?" She sounded disappointed.

"I must. But I can promise you if, in the end, the opportunity arises, you can make the kill." He blew the smoke out in one long exhale. He added a few smoke rings near the end.

A tingling sensation went from the top of Denise's head to her toes. She squirmed on Dimitri's chest.

"*Promise*?" She said enthusiastically.

"Of course, it's the least I can do." He took another drag.

"For putting out my eye?" She said with no malice.

"For helping me." He said as he held the smoke in his lungs.

Denise fell silent. It was an accident, after all. One training day, the practice with knives got out of control. They rolled, and Dimitri put her eye out with his blade in the ensuing struggle. The pain didn't come at first. There was just blood everywhere, and she had no idea where it was coming from. She thought that she had cut him deeply by accident. Her vision was blurry. She looked at him, and he looked at her. There was no expression on his face. He was unharmed. Slowly she brought her hand to her eye and gently touched the blood and aqueous humor oozing out of it. She felt light-headed and then outright dizzy. Blackness crept in. She woke up in the hospital. Dimitri never came to see her.

At first, She hated him with every fiber of her being after that. She had no idea where he had gone or how to find him. The revenge festered inside her for a long time. But as angry as she had been, she had missed him an equal amount. Now, lying in his arms, it seemed so far away. He was back in her life. She realized she would take him in whatever capacity the universe would allow. She thought either she would kill him one day or die for him.

"I am also going to murder Jared. He killed Marcos." He said very calmly and flatly.

Dimitri took another long drag of his cigarette. He held the smoke in as long as he could. He breathed out a very long stream of smoke. To this, Denise said nothing. There was nothing to say; she knew how Dimitri felt about Markos. A slight pang of jealousy swept over her. She shook it off. She would never have Dimitri, not in the way she needed.

"I will do that one myself in my own time. I just wanted you to know in case the North Koreans put a hit on him. He's mine. Do not interfere." He put his cigarette out in his palm.

"I wouldn't dream of it," Denise replied.

She continued to scratch his chest. She tried to snuggle in deeper. She couldn't get close enough to him. She was starting to doze. As she drifted off, she wondered, as she had for the millionth time...

Did Dimitri put her eye out on purpose?

# CHAPTER TWENTY-TWO

"Ph.D. CANDIDATE CRACKS CODE!"

THE NEWS EXPLODED all over the world.

Susan wasn't prepared for the onslaught. Reports swarmed her site; she found it impossible to get anything done. She was doing so many interviews. Her mentor insisted on it. It was excellent publicity for the college.

Good Morning America, Wired, The NY Times, Scientific American... even Sunday morning did a segment on her. The highlight of all of this for her was to be on late night with Andy. Her dream had not come true, it went well, and he did not transform into a monster. It was in the back of her mind during the entire interview.

"What does it say?" "Are they aliens?" "Is it true that they are advanced ancient humans?" The inquiries flooded in from everywhere.

The questions ranged from intelligent and thought-provoking to absurd. The emails were the most ridiculous. "What did they eat for breakfast" "Tell us about their fashion sense," and "Did they own pets?" That one got her, and she tried to find some evidence of this, but nothing so far. Most of what she was 'reading' was about science, exploration, politics, and philosophy.

That was the hardest part to explain. She wasn't reading the hieroglyphs; they were reading themselves to her. It was the ultimate form of communication. No effort is involved at all. She didn't have to learn the language; it was learning her. This is where she had made her mistake. She spent so much time trying to decipher the images that she didn't realize it was trying to figure out how it could 'decipher' her. That is why they appeared to move. Only through gamma brain waves can they be accessed. So, when she looked at them, she could hear what they meant in her head.

This became problematic. A portion of the population thought she was making things up. No one else could decipher them. You had to be close to them; a photograph was useless for decoding. Once it was decoded, she could disseminate the information. There was yet to be a discernible pattern she could make out. None of the repeating patterns are found in spoken languages. This made her job extremely difficult.

Then She had been sworn to secrecy by the British government on behalf of Jared. No one could know *how* she had figured out how to read the glyphs, lest another rival faction discovers how to gain entrance to the tower. And that is all they cared about. The pressure was immense. Between them constantly wanting updates on her progress and the interviews, she was getting nothing done. She felt they didn't believe her and that she was holding back. But she wasn't. It wasn't there anywhere, on any building surface in the complex. At least not yet, anyway. Maybe she needed to find the actual door. Who knew?

At this point, she did not care. Her mission had been accomplished. She had cracked the code to an amazingly beautiful and complex language, and she reveled in that. She had defended her thesis and was now a full-fledged doctor. She had seen the gentleman in the bar again and was developing a relationship with him. They were dating, if it could be called that. She loved his Russian accent. Her new friend Denise had introduced them. She was from Portugal, and Susan enjoyed practicing her Portuguese with her. It felt good to have a friend again, someone with whom she could chat about more normal things, such as shopping, shows, and men. A much-needed break from all the serious science and interviews. They just met, drank, chatted, and laughed.

She was working on a book about her adventures, in secret, of course. She was writing in her private moments in her shack at night. The rest of her time was spent with her research and writing everything down that the language told her. It was beautiful in that it almost knew her questions before she asked them. It presented knowledge to her when her mind wandered in that direction. One day she had spent the entire day learning about the planets they had traveled to within the solar system and the different bases and cultures that developed on different moons. The knowledge seemed limitless, and she couldn't absorb it fast enough. It was consuming her.

Charles and his workforce had set up a workshop around her area. She was simply at the wall of the tower, at its base. The words were appearing on the alabaster surface faster than anyone could read. To the other observers, nothing was happening. The hieroglyphs just seemed to simmer or change. It was a beautiful dance to Susan, and she recorded it all digitally. There were different hieroglyphs at different points of the base of the tower, but she had yet to work out their significance. They were working their way around the base. This one spot was over-whelming her with science. That suited her just fine, more than enough for a life's work.

British intelligence continued to pressure her for more. They were not interested in the history of these people nor where they went, or what they did. They wanted to know how they did it. So, they colonized Titan, so what? How did they do it? How did they get there? What was the power source? Where were the diagrams? Where were the precious diagrams? Where were the schematics? Where were the *weapons,* Susan thought? That was all that they were interested in. Getting a foothold on taking over the world again. Being in charge, a world power. Returning to their old slogan, "The sun does not set on the Union Jack." So transparent. She didn't care if she ever got into the tower; this was enough to keep her busy for the rest of her life. Even if she did get in, which would be nice, she wasn't sure she wanted to. She wasn't so sure if she did find out how to do it, she would tell them.

Charles stood outside as a guard; no one got in without his permission. He hardly left her side or was out of sight. She had become too important, and she knew that MI6 had assigned Jared to watch her every move on the site. It got to the point where she was so used to him being there that it felt strange when he wasn't around. As she worked, he sat in the room at his computer and didn't bother her, but she knew he was recording her every move. Getting alone time with Dimitri was next to impossible, but she managed it somehow. He was an excellent lover, attentive and giving. He didn't require anything of her but her company. That was a pleasant escape because it seemed everyone wanted something from her. Everyone.

"I don't like that Russian," Charles said, "He seems... a little too oily to me. Like a slippery eel."

"Don't be jealous, Chuck, it's unbecoming," Susan said playfully; she was in a good mood.

"It's not that, and you know it." Chuck retorted, 'You're like a sister to me, and I don't want to see you get hurt.' He was rubbing his hands together.

"Chuckles, you are so sweet" Susan grabbed his beard and, on her tiptoes, made him bend over for a kiss on the cheek. "I know that you are just doing your job."

"And you are *not* making it easy for me. You are always trying to sneak off with him and lose me in the process." He was brooding now.

"It is such a fun game, isn't it?" She giggled.

"No, it is not." He grumbled.

Dimitri entered the room. "Am I interrupting?" He said as he took Susan's hand in his and kissed it.

"*No/Yes.*" Susan and Charles said, in that order at the same time.

"How nice to see you again, Mr. Holiki." Dimitri smiled at him.

Charles did not move, looking him in the eye. He may have had murder on his mind. Dimitri met his gaze unflinchingly. Neither made a move to shake the other's hand. Jared didn't look up; he did not make eye contact. Dimitri knew he was there and ignored him. His time would come. He was a patient man, extremely patient. He could feel the cold sweat coming from Jared every time they were in the same room.

He loved it; he relished it. Soon my friend, soon, I will end you like you ended Marco.

Dimitri turned to Susan. "Are you ready for dinner?"

"Yes, let's have some fun!" She said brightly.

And with that, they spun on their heels and left the field lab.

Charles grunted, and Jared finally let his breath out.

"I hate that guy..." They both said in unison.

They looked at each other and laughed.

# CHAPTER TWENTY-THREE

TANAKA SPAT AT HIS HOLOSCREEN. The spit flew through the holographic image right through Susan's forehead and hit the wall behind. The show's host, Andy, didn't seem to notice. What did that Jew know about aliens? An ancient human race? What was that rubbish? He shut off the device and paced around his makeshift shack. He was in contact with them. Had been for years. When the tower started to slowly reveal itself, he knew, he knew right away that it was left there by them before they left. He knew because they had told him. Yes, he could talk to them. It's why he left Nagoya to come to the 'True Believers' section of Tower Town. He was tired of watching her go on and on about something she was obviously making up. She was a charlatan, and he hated her for it.

The Grays had started abducting him when he was a child, seven to be exact. He had many memories of the experiments that they put him through. They were his only family. Growing up an orphan in Japan was not easy. He looked forward to being taken away. He felt it made him special, needed... important. They came to him in dreams, often. He had entire conversations with them. He felt like one of them. They hadn't taken him in some time, but that didn't matter; he was going to get into the tower, find a ship, and go to them. He knew one had to be in there.

They told him to go inside, explaining how to get in. He needed to possess a very precious and specific item at the top of the tower. It was of utmost importance. They wanted him to follow the doctor into the tower when she unlocked it. They wanted him to murder her. They wanted the object. He wanted the ship. They told him where it was. They would tell him how to fly it once he found it, and the real adventure of his life would start. He would be off this filthy planet with all the filthy human inhabitants that had destroyed it with their greed and aversiveness. They promised him the ability to explore the universe and its marvelous mysteries if only he brought them the orb.

Tanaka had never known such purpose or singularity of mind. Find a way in, kill the doctor, find the orb, get in the ship, deliver the prize and live a life he had dreamed of since he was a child. He made his way to the center of the 'True Believers' section of the tower town. The middle had a golden statue of a Gray looking majestic. So many freaks and geeks were in various states of prayer, trance, or chanting. They had formed a circle around the statue, but it never dispersed. Since he came, there has been a 24/7/365 congregation around it. Some wore sackcloth and burned incense. Others wore crystals or tin foil hats. Others sat in silence. A few crazies stood on the edge shouting about the end of the world and to repent. A few Buddhist monks or Jesuit priests could be spotted, and Tanaka wondered if they knew something everyone else didn't. There was always a very low hum of human voices he couldn't quite put his finger on, like an ohm but more of a buzz. It was strangely pleasant to him.

The smell of roasting flesh caught his nose, and his stomach rumbled. He made his way over to the food district with a skip in his step. He was smiling broadly. None of these fools knew the truth as he did. They were all deluded and would be stuck on this rock in the thick of this muck while he was exploring nebulae and rings and asteroids and black holes. He laughed out loud. A voice in his head said; 'remember, you MUST kill the doctor or there will be no ship. She cannot be in possession of the orb.' Tanaka knew his purpose. For so long he pined for the Grays to take him away for good. Every time he woke from an abduction to find himself on Earth, he wept. Now was his chance. He would prove his worth to them. He would be equal. He would be a star trekker.

Nothing else mattered to him.

# CHAPTER TWENTY-FOUR

JARED LEANED back in his chair. Chuck had said something about going to do something vague. Probably following Susan again. Jared didn't know why he tortured himself. Chuck would never have her. Then again, did he want her in that way? Maybe it was more like a big brother's worry. He never caught Charles looking at her in any way resembling lust. He could tell that he loved her. That was painfully obvious. She was charming and adorable, and smart. He could tell Chuck had it bad. It was deep. Maybe the fact that she was spending so much time with Dimitri and not him bothered him. Chuck did say that he didn't trust Dimitri. Jared sighed. What was he doing? Why hadn't Dimitri tried to kill him? There is absolutely no way that he has forgiven him for putting a hole in the middle of his friend's chest at point-blank range. And why hadn't he told HQ about Dimitri? They had to know... anyway, screw them; he wasn't telling them anything. Still, he was no further along in his own goal of blowing this entire thing to hell.

He needed to be inside for that to happen. That didn't seem like it was happening anytime soon. Susan was pleased to research, write papers, go on interviews and translate to her heart's content. No amount of prodding on his part (or from MI6) was getting her to move faster. She even told him as much. She didn't care if she ever got inside.

"What's in there that is so important? Do you need to use the restroom or something? Get off my back about it." Besides, as much as it chafed his ass, it wasn't up to her. It was up to that old Buddha alien thing. Jared had talked Susan into the machine once. She was sick of him asking her to do it. She conceded, and nothing happened. She just sat there with a blissful smile on her face. When she got up, she just looked at him and walked out. He later found out she was in a beautiful garden with talking animals and plants. What the heck? Ugh.

He had also tried the machine himself again. Nothing. He didn't have the brain matter, the patience, or whatever it was that Susan had that no one else seemed to possess. He had a theory that it was her life-long study of languages that gave her the ability to communicate with the aliens. She had formed her brain differently over the years. Or was she "the chosen one"? No one had come right out and said it, but he had his suspicions. Maybe he was a dirty old alien trying to get into her pants? Nah, that was a stupid thought. Jared may not have been the brightest crayon in the box, but he knew there was more at play here than simply getting laid. It had been a while for him. His mind was wandering... A trip to the red section of the circle would ease his tension. He could use a massage with a happy ending.

He contemplated walking out into the middle of the town circle and detonating the vest every now and then. Just go for it. Vaporize everyone and everything, including himself, in one blissful instant. Once, he almost did. He was so close, his finger on the pull ring, index finger wrapped around it. He wasn't depressed. He wasn't mad. He was just... bored. All this waiting around recording everything Susan did, and reporting back was getting old. And the constant leering of Dimitri was driving him mad. One day, as he walked towards his favorite fish roasting kiosk, he saw Dimitri with that smug look. Jared was literally pulling on the ring in his vest before he knew it. He was going to stare Dimitri in the eyes as he tore every atom out of his body with one swift motion. But Chuck came up behind him, slapped him on the shoulder, and scared the heck out of him. They went and got a drink; none knew how close they were to not existing.

Despite himself, he was starting to like Charles, sort of... the conversation wasn't great. Chuck was a blue-collar man through and through.

Hard work was his religion. He was constantly working on some machine or creating something in his workshop. Jared found himself spending more time than he liked with him. If Susan wasn't shutting out the world with her headphones on, deep into research or translating, she was with Dimitri or Denise. He laughed to himself; he'd have more luck getting Charles into the Gamma inducer than her. So much for that plan. The best he could do was bide his time and hope he was with her when she gained entry. She made no bones about not liking him. At. All.

No, the conversations were about automobiles, sports, mostly rugby, the girl back home that got away, or stupid adventures growing up. This was all done rather loudly and obnoxiously over a drink at the 'The Cooler.' The drunker Chuck got, the louder he got. The constant slapping him on the shoulder or back was growing wearisome. He knew it was Chuck's way of showing affection, but he developed an ache in his trapezius muscle. A knot was there now that would not go away. Hence another reason to hit the red sector for some deep tissue therapy. He guessed that they were developing some kind of male bonding thing. He had never had that, so he didn't know what that was like. The closest thing he had to a friend was Nigel back home. That was all, Nigel. He was the one that would call and get him out of the apartment. He never regretted it, Nigel had style, but he would never have initiated it.

Before he knew it, he was up and out of the research area and winding his way down the narrow streets of the circle, headed to the massage parlor on autopilot. Smells and sounds and sights would have blasted anyone else's senses. Jared was oblivious. Absentmindedly he dodged the denizens of the makeshift shanty town and found himself in front of an unassuming unmarked door made of rusted metal and wood. He knocked and waited. After a moment, it slowly creaked open. A tiny woman appeared seemingly out of thin air.

"Mr. Jared, do come in." She said in a soft voice. She was bowing, hands in prayer.

He did as bidden and followed her to the back. Her silken robes showed her every curve, but loosely. It seemed alive as she walked smoothly, almost gliding. The smell of incense and oils replaced the smell of charred animal flesh from outside. Unconsciously he breathed it in deeply, absorbing as much as he could. Upon entering his private room, he escaped his attire and lay on the table face down. He waited.

He heard her small hands pumping oil into them and being rubbed together. She immediately went to his left shoulder and his knot. She dug in deep, and Jared eased into it.

What was he doing? What was going on? He hadn't a clue. He was just going through the motions lately. Something better happen soon, or he would pull that pin out.

He was.

It was simply a matter of time. With the thought of his atoms finally becoming one with the source again, he dozed off as the masseuse worked out his tension.

# CHAPTER TWENTY-FIVE

DENISE once again found herself alone at the back of the bar, seething. She thought that she would be ok with Dimitri and Susan, but feelings have a mind of their own. It was the mission, after all. Susan didn't mean anything to him. He was just playing with her, milking her for information. But as Denise nursed her drink and got drunker as the evening passed, a thought crept into her mind. That thought was a small seed that was being nurtured by alcohol. As she fed it, it grew. That thought was that she wasn't good enough. That was the trunk, the base of that thought. Its roots went deep into her abusive childhood. It had branches, and they were reaching out, filling with the light of jealousy. One particular branch gaining momentum was the thought that Ditrimi was falling in love with Susan. As she watched them, she could see how he looked at her. It was different. He had never looked at her that way. It was the way he kept touching her, over and over. It was maddening. And he laughed way too hard at her jokes or anything else she said. He hung on every word. By her 5th scotch, Denise was sure Dimitiri was in love with Susan. She just knew it.

What she didn't know was what she would do about it. She could just kill Dimitri and be done with it. In her inebriated state, that seemed the simplest solution to her conundrum. No Dimitri, no pain, no jealousy... no nothing. Done. Another branch that was growing off of her truck of self-loathing was that she should do away with her romantic rival. She liked Susan; she genuinely did, considered her a girlfriend even. But business was business, and she still wanted Dimitri. What pained her the most was she wasn't invited to the party. She had hoped on some level that she would have them both. When she asked, suggesting a three-some could be fun for all, Dimitri coldly refused her. He said that Susan would never go for it. Denise had her doubts. She was convinced that Dimitri had changed and Susan had changed him. That he wanted her all to himself and that he was no longer interested in her. By this point, the drinks had set her tree on fire, and she could literally feel smoke coming off her. She had never felt such rage or jealousy. What was wrong with her? She was better than this. What was it about this man that drove her to madness?

As she watched them flirt, laugh, and touch each other, her head began to swim. She had a choice to make. Ruin everything, the mission, the money, the possibility of being with Dimitri and her friendship with Susan, or sit tight and play this hand out to the bitter end. She was seriously having doubts, especially the part about betraying Susan. It had never bothered her before. She had befriended many and then, literally, put a knife in their backs and happily collected her paycheck. This was different. All of those bastards deserved it one way or the other. She slept well at night, knowing they got what was coming to them. She was making the world a better place in her own twisted way. The world was certainly better off without those evil people. Susan was different. She had a gift, she was making a difference, and Denise *liked* her. Damn it all to hell. Knowing Dimitri, it would end in death. It always did. Denise wasn't sure she could live with Susan's death on her hands, even if she didn't pull the trigger.

Denise decided that she was through feeling sorry for herself and that the self-loathing pity party was over. She needed to work this drunk off somehow. Her eyes settled on the bartender she had noticed upon arriving here the first time. He was still working away, but he was stealing an occasional glance her way, looking for permission to come in for a landing. Denise decided to flag him in. Staring at him intently, she let her finger slide around the top of her glass, doing her best 'come hither look. It didn't take long.

"Wanna get out of here, big boy?" She said in her sexiest voice.

"Yes ma'am, I do." and with that, he turned around.

"Hey, Kurtus! I am going to take a break." He yelled.

He threw his dish rag at Kurt, who deftly caught it. Kurt winked at the bartender and nodded, a code between long-time coworkers.

Denise stood up, and he walked around the bar, extending his arm, which she took happily. She would need the support; the scotch was hitting hard. They walked out of the bar arm and arm. She made it a point to walk past Susan and Dimitri. She didn't look over, but she could feel their eyes on her as she passed.

She waited until she was outside to smile.

# CHAPTER TWENTY-SIX

CHARLES AND JARED were at the other end of the bar. Chuck had made sure to take a table so he could see Susan. There were other people at the table when they arrived. Charles stood over them, casting a shadow, silent, but his request was clear. When one of them noticed him, without saying a word, he hit the shoulder of the guy next to him, and they both stood up and moved on. Rather quickly too. Jared thought this man did have his uses.

Charles made eye contact with Kurtus, and the usual drinks followed shortly. He downed the first one in one fell swoop and slammed it on the table; Jared was used to this by now. He made no signs of noticing. He picked up the next pint. He commenced leering in Susan's direction, taking another swig of his ale, and said.

"I really hate guys like him," Charles grunted as some beer dripped off his beard. He didn't seem to notice.

Jared rolled his eyes; here we go again...

"Really good-looking guys get on my nerves. Women fall all over them, and they have this holier-than-thou attitude." He looked at Jared accusingly.

He took another swig and wiped his red beard with the back of his hand.

"Come on, man, look at you! You are a paragon of masculinity." Jared spat. "You're like that Men at Work song, six foot four and full of muscle. What have you got to complain about? You look like a mountain, for chrissakes." Jared said, exasperated.

"Whatever." Charles took another long draw, finished it, and slammed that one on the table. Two more ales appeared out of nowhere as if on cue. Jared turned just in time to see Kurtus retreating to the bar.

"I think you are jealous," Jared said sardonically.

"Bah!" Chuck locked his gaze on Jared.

Jared returned the stare unflinchingly. He just didn't care anymore.

"Come on, admit it. You got it bad for Susan." Jared took a sip of his ale and looked at Charles through his glass mug for his reaction.

Charles grumbled, "No, that's not it at all. She's like my sister, you knucklehead. I *care* about her. Deeply. She reminds me of Tracy, my younger sister. I lost her in a stupid scuba diving accident." As soon as he said it, he regretted it.

Jared was silent. He waited for Chuck to continue. He took a noisy sip of his beer. Still looking at him through the glass mug.

Charles was looking ahead at nothing. Jared knew he was there, remembering the moment it happened. It was written all over his face. Was that a tear forming in the corner of his eye?

Charles could feel Jared's eyes on him, waiting. Would he share the story of how he failed his sister? Of how she drowned, inches away, right in front of him. He didn't know if he could bear it. He didn't know if he even liked Jared enough to tell him. This guy was so shut down. Why in the world would he want to open up to him? Would Jared even care? He saw Jared just looking at him balefully, with no expression, sipping on his ale. Deep in his soul, he had this feeling that Dimitri was rotten to the core. He didn't know why he felt it. He didn't dare tell Susan either; she seemed so happy, and smiling so much more lately. Everything was going her way. Besides, she would just call him jealous again and wave him off.

Charles took a deep breath and sighed. He proceeded to tell Jared how he and his sister were dive buddies and urban treasure hunters. Deep sea rescue certified. She was younger and full of piss and vinegar. She was always taking chances on their salvage dives. This particular job was in an office building, deep in the lower levels. There was a rumor of an old vault with safety deposit boxes full of gems, jewels, etc. You know, that one last haul mythos of treasure hunters. Tracy had heard about it from a former bank employee of that building. The old Teller said they'd be set for life if anyone could get down there and get it out. It was in Baltimore, the Old Court Savings and Loan building. They didn't know how deep it was, but they knew it would be dark, cold, and dangerous, but worth a look. They took a month to plan it. Got the blueprints from some hacker online and organized the gear needed to do an extended dive. The first dive was just reconnaissance. They didn't bring any torches or bolt cutters, or lock picks. Just headlamps and a thirst for adventure and exploration.

Jared was actually on the edge of his seat, listening to Chuck. He had always wanted to dive. He took another long draw of his ale and leaned in to hear more.

"The day started off well enough as we motored our boat out to the inner city of Baltimore. Our GPS put us right over the building. It was entirely submerged. We weighed the anchor. We were going to do the dive in stages with tanks at different levels waiting for us as we came back up for some decompression time. We knew how deep the water was, so we lowered the tanks to the bottom (that's street level), put on our dry suits, and hit the water. It's surreal free falling in water past floors of a building", Chuck commented. He continued, "We got to street level, made sure our spare tanks were set and proceeded to the door. Access was not a problem, and we made our way to the elevator shaft. Another easy form of access, our luck was with us; the elevator was stationed above us three floors. We dove down and hit the bottom level. Took a bit to get there."

Chuck stopped for a drink. He upended the mug and swallowed in one fluid motion. He slammed it down harder than ever, and Jared thought it would smash. He knew what was coming next. He realized he was holding his breath and slowly let it out so he wouldn't break Charle's stride. The suspense was killing him. When the new mugs appeared from Kurtus, he also took a long drink.

"The vault was right there. Beautiful, big, round with a flat bottom and *open*. We couldn't believe our luck. Three strokes in a row. Most, if not all, of the safety deposit boxes were intact. Tracy went in first, and I searched around the outside. Before I knew it, the portcullis closed with a click, and she was locked inside the vault. To this day I still have no idea how it happened. Did she hit it with her fin? Was it just disturbed? As hard as I could pull, it would not open. I broke my dive knife trying to pry it open as well. We didn't panic; we've been in worse situations. We worked on the problem but to no avail. We were DEEP, and you use air quicker. Besides, we didn't plan on staying long; we were looking around to see if it was worth a more serious commitment. Time and air were running out, and we had to decide quickly. I told her that I would go back to the ground level and get her a spare and bring it down, then go to the surface and get a torch and burn the lock."

Charles could see Jared's confused look.

"We were using full face masks with microphones." he said.

Jared was green by this time. He thought he might actually throw up. He couldn't take another sip.... "Jesus, then what?" He hissed.

"She said 'No, you'll get the bends; you won't make it.' She pointed at me. She shook her head violently." Chuck whispered.

"I told her I did't give a fuck. She wasn't dying today.

She was adamant. 'You won't make it.' was all she said over and over."

Charles was openly crying at this point.

"She knew that I would die with her, that I wouldn't go anywhere without her, she knew I would breathe my last breath with her... so ... she..." He trailed off and couldn't get the words out.

"No..." Jared whispered.

After composing himself, he went on.

"Yes, she backed away from the gate and pulled out her dive knife. 'I love you brother,' was the last thing she said to me. She then took off her face mask and cut the hose connected to it. She floated still for what seemed like an eternity holding her breath. I was going mad, banging on the gate. Her scuba tank air was bleeding freely to the vaults ceiling. Finally, her eyes got so wide... I'll never forget it, and she breathed in. And for a moment, a look of utter calm came over her. She breathed the water a few more times, and then, she was gone. I could see it in her eyes.

There was nothing there." Charles was weeping by this time, sobbing silently. His head was in his hands.

Jared did something he had never done before. He reached out and put his hand on Chuck's shoulder to comfort him. Say what you want about the big lug, he had a heart, and it was torn out that day.

Charles looked up. There was a silent understanding between them.


Things had changed.

# CHAPTER TWENTY-SEVEN

SUSAN'S FACE HURT. She hadn't smiled or laughed this much in her entire life. Dimitri was delightful. What she liked best about him was that he didn't seem to want anything from her. Which, in turn, made her want to give him everything. He was charming, articulate, kind, thoughtful, funny, and damn good-looking. The fact that he was a generous lover with incredible stamina didn't hurt either. And that accent, she could listen to him talk all day. She had never had a relationship like this. It was relaxed and laid back, with no expectations. He had told her earlier that his mission was to have fun and enjoy each other's company. She found this refreshing. So many past lovers were so possessive. They wanted something. It was all so conditional. He was so calm, like a Buddhist zen master. Nothing fazed him. He had a demeanor that was calming to be around. He planned things for them to do. Also, he wasn't paranoid or didn't seem to have any anxiety to speak of. He was never controlling and happy to do whatever she wished. Why couldn't every man be this way? Why all the unnecessary drama? "Girls just wanna have fun!" has been running over and over in her mind lately. Cindy had it right.

"So, tell me, Susan, how was your latest interview with Wired Magazine? What did they ask you that didn't make it into the interview?"

Dimitri liked having the details. If only she knew that he was fishing for information to enter the tower.

Susan also appreciated that he listened and reflected on her. She felt heard and understood.

"They kept asking me if I would ever figure out how to open the Tower. They were singularly obsessed with that and kept going on about how there must be amazing ancient technology. What if we could access it? It would transform our lives and maybe even heal the planet. So much speculation we have no idea if there is anything inside that tower that could help us at all. I am just happy to work on my translations and learn more about these people." She said this as she was sipping her wine. She continued.

"Then the interviewer asked me if I wasn't curious about the aliens that might be inside. Dead or alive.." Susan knew better than to tell anyone about her 'alien' dreams, especially Dimitri. She liked him; she certainly didn't want him to run screaming.

"I had to patiently explain that the only evidence we have found of their species was the body at the base, and he was mostly human, not an alien. You know, you would be amazed at how many times I have had to explain that. It's like people want it to be aliens, that an ancient society smarter than ours is unthinkable." She put her glass down and looked at the ceiling contemplating this.

"Well, why not ask? Even if they don't understand. Sounds pretty darn fascinating to me." He leaned back in his chair, took a sip of his bourbon, and looked at her challengingly.

"Not really. I never gave much credence to aliens in the first place. People interest me much more than a hypothetical alien in another world we're unlikely ever to encounter. If there is anything in the tower? It's probably ancient humans who had advanced tech. We are smart; we figure things out pretty quickly. And we forget and get distracted and have wars and disasters; anything could have happened to them. Unfortunately, technology inherently has the seeds of its own destruction within it. As a scientist, I am trying to distance myself from that religious crowd at the base of the tower who seem to believe the tower was built by aliens?... They tend to be wackadoos. I had a boyfriend who was way into ancient aliens and all that stuff. It used to upset me that he didn't think humans were smart enough to make the wonders of the world. That it had to be some outside benevolent force from a distant star who built the great ancient structures of Earth. We built the bloody pyramids. Just because we don't know how we did, doesn't mean we didn't. I hated that." She finished her wine and motioned to the waiter for another.

Dimitri mused over this for a few moments. After a few moments of reflection, he spoke.

"I have a friend with a similar theory. He states that aliens were actually an evolved form of us from long ago. Hence the same features, the ability to breathe our atmosphere and withstand our gravity. Basically, the grays were us gone mad with pushing tech too far. They are still here on Earth and on other planets within our solar system. He said that stars are just way too far apart for travel between them. He didn't believe in F.T.L. travel or warp fields. Any intelligent life evolving on a different planet would be incredibly different than here. His argument was that the grays are our distant relatives because life from another star would not resemble us at all. Seems that your research is giving this theory some credence?" He looked at her expectantly.

This was another reason why Susan liked Dimitri so much. He was intelligent and could carry on a compelling conversation without being nuts.

"Yes, it seems that way. The civilization here did have larger than normal craniums and extremely advanced technology. The proof of that is the language and the tower itself. They were very similar to the Grays. Fetu says that the grays came from them..." As soon as the words left her mouth, she was sorry they did. Her guard was down, and she had a good buzz going.

"Fetu?" Dimitri asked.

"Nothing. I have no idea what I meant by that; it must be the drinks working on me." She looked down sheepishly.

"Are you getting all mystical on me?" he teased.

"No! Not at all, just some crazy dream I had..." she was flustered and was trying to regain her composure.

"Tell me about it." He leaned in, putting his elbows on the table.

"Well... I dunno... it's silly." She looked away.

"No, it's not, it's important to me." He said with total sincerity.

"It is?" She was taken aback a little.

"Yes, I care about you Susan and the things that you do. Your research is endlessly fascinating." He took another drink and swirled the alcohol within it.

Susan blushed. That was nice to hear; it's been a while. She proceeded to tell him about the Elder and how he was always in a lotus position floating a few inches off the ground, and he seemed to be directing her towards... something. She didn't know what to make of it; he seemed so real. She had this strange feeling that she would meet him soon.

Dimitri rubbed his stubbed chin. He looked at her pensively.

"HHhhhhhmmmm... I wonder if it's some form of telepathy?" He said this slowly, carefully, and thoughtfully.

"Now you're talking like one of those wackadoos. No such thing; I don't believe in that. There is absolutely no science to it." She tried not to sound defensive.

"There is more to life than meets the eye, Susan. Science doesn't have all the answers." He winked.

"Well, for me, it does, and that's that." She put her drink down to indicate that was the end of the discussion.

"As you wish." And with that, he dropped the topic.

Another thing she appreciated about him, he was flexible without being defensive. She took another sip of her drink and looked at him.

"Do you wanna get out of here?" She was feeling good, the alcohol was warm and pleasing.

Dimitri saw the look in her eye and how her finger was tracing the rim of her glass.

"Yes, that would be lovely."

# CHAPTER TWENTY-EIGHT

TONIGHT WAS the night that Tanaka was going to carry out his plan. Tonight was the night that he was going to murder Susan while she walked home from 'The Cooler.' He had been stalking her for weeks. She had a pattern. It was the weekend, so she would have been drinking and less guarded. She would not be on her toes. She would be in the alleyway that she took on her way home. He knew that she would be with that mountain man too. He would end her and him and take his place among the Grays. They came to him last night in a dream. He knew it wasn't a dream; he knew that they had really abducted him this time. But this time, there was no torture, experiments, probing, or removal of bodily fluids or sperm. They talked to him. They talked to him in his mind. They told him that Susan was close to entering the tower. Close to taking the thing that they most coveted. That it must never be released. Humans should never possess the orb. It would ruin everything. They told him that his reward would be great. That he would travel the stars like them, as equals.

Tanaka's excitement was fever-pitched. He cleaned his gun for the last time tonight. After this, they would probably give him a ray gun or something. Maybe even a disintegration ray. He could hardly contain himself; his glee was so acute. Finally, he had permission. Finally, he had the courage. All the nights of torture of being without his surrogate Gray parents would end. Finally, he would be free to roam the galaxy, seek new life and civilizations, and boldly go where no one has gone before. He would join them and show them what he was made of.

He put the gun in his pocket, zipped up his parka, and braved the cold air. He made his way to the spot he had picked out earlier for his ambush. They had said that she was dangerous, that he had to take her by surprise. The big man was also no one to be trifled with; this had to be quick. He didn't think she would be any trouble at all; she was so small. He could easily handle her. But, it was better to listen to the masters; they always knew best. He hid behind the dumpsters and waited. Not long now, and her and his fate would be sealed.

It reeked. He was behind two dumpsters, side by side. Just enough room between them so that he could stand in front of her quickly when she passed by, put a bullet in her and her Samoan companion's chest, and walk away. It was dark; Antarctica was in the throes of its half-year-long twilight. No one would see him; hardly anyone would notice two shots in this shanty town; they happened all the time. They would just be the victims of a random robbery. He had to remember to take her i-wallet-watch and something else from the large one to make it look like a hold-up gone wrong. The ground was slippery with grease, and he was positive that what he felt around his ankle were rats sniffing him out. He didn't dare move. He just hoped that they didn't find him tasty. He could feel the tanto dagger against his back in his belt, there for backup, just in case.

He heard walking in the distance. His heart began to race. He listened closely. There were two sets of footsteps. She wasn't alone. He could hear a Russian voice with her. This wasn't the giant. What to do? What to do? He was going to go for it. The clip was full, if he had to use two rounds in quick succession, then so be it. The Grays said that it had to be tonight. Nothing would stand in his way. He was on his haunches now, ready to pounce. The voices were getting closer. Any second now. He was actually sweating. A bead rolled down his nose.

He saw the shadows first and knew it was now or never. He moved like a cat, all the years of Aikikai at the brutal dojo in Nagoya came forward. He was in front of them both in an instant but too close. He didn't have time to think about which one to shoot first, but Susan was definitely the priority. Before he knew what was happening, she had stepped to the side and held his hand with the gun, and she smoothly moved behind him, still holding on, executing a beautiful kotegaeshi throw. The gun went off. It was terribly loud in the silence of the alleyway, and the flash from its mussel was blinding in the dark. The bullet ricocheted off the concrete pavement. Tanaka went end over end and rolled out of the hold. Susan did manage to get the gun from him, but it slipped out of her hand as he came up immediately to counter her. The gun slid and stopped at the toe of Dimitri's shoe.

Dimitri reached to pick up the gun, but before she could grab it, Tanaka rose up, a tanto in his hand, thrusting towards Susan's midsection. Dimitri, not having time to place his finger on the trigger, raised the gun in an arching motion and caught Tanaka on the chin. It was a glancing blow but saved Susan from a belly full of steel. This gave her the opening she needed. With his chin in the air, she planted her fist into his Adam's apple as hard as she could, she was in a solid stance, and the force pushed her back a little, sliding on the grease by the dumpster. Tanaka gasped for air, grabbing his throat as he fell backward.

He landed on his ass with a plop, the tanto falling between his legs. Dimitri simply stood to one side with the gun trained on Tanaka. He waited for Susan's next move. This was her show. Susan looked at Tanaka with fire in her eyes as she slowly brought herself out of her fighting stance. He was gradually catching his breath. She had wondered if she crushed his windpipe, but the greasy street had spared his life. No one said a word. Tanaka slowly got onto his knees and sat in seiza, breathing heavily. He started to untuck his shirt slowly without losing eye contact with Susan as he reached for the blade between his knees.

Both she and Dimitri knew what was coming next.

Tanaka knew it was over, he was caught, and there would not any prize tonight. There would be no glorious reunion with the Grays. No ship. No trekking through the stars. If they didn't kill him now, he would be dragged to prison, and it would be a circus; he just tried to assassinate the doctor that translated the tower language. She was a celebrity. He couldn't face the shame. He did what any self-respecting samurai would do. He would commit seppuku. He looked to Dimitri and then back to Susan.

"Jinsei wa yumedearu!"

He plunged the knife into his belly as far as it would go and started to drag it to the side, disemboweling himself. Susan did not flinch nor lose eye contact. He coughed, and blood came out of his mouth, a deep, dark red. His insides spilled all over the greasy alley. He turned to Dimitri with a pleading look.

Dimitri understood. He walked up to Tanaka and placed the gun on his forehead.

Tanaka closed his eyes.

From a distance, a large crack and a flash of light appeared.


Then, silence.

# CHAPTER TWENTY-NINE

"YOU BURNED SOMEONE *ALIVE*," Charles immediately snapped out of his revelry.

"It was an *accident...*" Jared took another sip of his beer and looked away, suddenly embarrassed.

"Ok..." Chuck also took another drink and looked at Jared, waiting for some kind of explanation.

Jared was quiet for a while. "I am really sorry about your sister. That totally sucks, man," he whispered.

"Thank you." Charles seemed appreciative.

"Did you go back for her? The treasure? Anything?" Jared was still very curious.

"Yes, all of it. I'm pretty well off. I am just here because I like work, and to keep my hands busy. The Tower is a huge draw; I had to see it for myself. I gave her a proper burial. The cash out was substantial after the government stepped in and made sure to return the valuables to the proper owners and collect their taxes. There was a "finders/salvage fee." Got me my new legs. But you are changing the subject. I need to know what happened if I am to sit at the same table with you." Charles was gripping his mug tightly.

"I am not sure if telling you will make it any better or the reason why." Jared was looking down into his beer.

"I still need to know. *Now.*" Charles demanded. He had a mind to just get up and leave, but he was too curious.

Jared looked into his mug and started. "It's not well known, but I was an eco-terrorist. My specialty was blowing up gas stations. I was part of the Green Liberation Front." There was a touch of pride in his voice. He believed that he was making a difference.

"I've heard of them. Eco fanatics. 'The ends justify the means type of group, right? *'If they won't play, they will pay.'* Wasn't that your motto? At first, I had a kind of respect for your group, but people *died,* and that's no good." He looked Jared in the eye as he said this, putting emphasis on 'died.'

Jared sighed, "Yes, they did, but never on my missions. My goal was zero deaths. We had some in our faction that just didn't care who got hurt. They slept at night because they blamed it on the oil companies' greed and that they were making us all sick, poisoning the planet. The car companies kept their promise by changing over to all-electric by 2030. It wasn't enough. There were still gas engines, trucks, airplanes, cargo ships... we wanted change now."

"So, your answer was to blow up as many gas stations and fuel depots as possible?" Chuck snorted. "You guys were a problem, you made a huge mess."

"Yes, we did. We felt it was justified payback.", Jared said defensively.

Charles ignored this. "So, what happened on your mission?"

"I was to hit a local convenience store gas station. One of my cohorts was to call in a bomb scare. It would vacate the building, and in between the time it took for the authorities to arrive, I would detonate my charges. We were taken seriously at the time, so when people got the call, they ran." Jared drank a long pull from his mug.

"And?" Charles asked.

"And there was a guy there that just didn't leave... I dunno why or what he was doing, but as I pushed the plunger, he was walking out of the bathroom. I guess they forgot about him, or he didn't hear. Crap. The blast just hit him in a way, you know? The flames engulfed him, and he lit up like a match. At first, he didn't seem to notice. But then he started to run. He took one breath in, and that was that. He fell to his knees, and I watched his flesh melt in front of me. I was done. It wasn't long after that, that the British government caught me. I think I wanted to be caught. I couldn't sleep for a long time and still have nightmares." Jared put his drink down in defeat.

"You didn't go to prison?" Charles said incredulously.

"No, Mi6 had other plans for me. Being a celebrity of some sort and a scientist gave them the advantage to find others and use me in other ways. I gave up my entire team. The government said that I was not only facing a slew of charges, least of all arson and manslaughter, but treason. They cure that one by hanging." Jared sat back in his chair and rubbed his temples. "I betrayed everyone."

"You're Mi6?!" Charles roared with laughter. "A spy? Are you licensed to kill too, James?"

This slight hurt a bit, but Jared took it in stride.

"Well... if I do happen to kill someone, it could be overlooked, per se." And he looked at Chuck. Chuck stopped dead and returned his gaze.

"Unlike Dimitri, that bastard can kill with impunity. He's F.S.K. " Jared spat.

"What? What did you just say?" This time he really had Charles's attention.

Jared was immediately silent. He knew right away that he had messed up. Damned alcohol... Charles did not know about Dimitri. He had explicit instructions not to reveal him to anyone. As far as Mi6 was concerned, Dimitris' meddling was moving their case forward. He was to simply observe and report. Not take action. Not to tell.

By this time, Chuck had Jared by the throat, in the air and his feet were off the ground. Jared could smell his hot alcohol breath. He was across the table. and his chair was knocked over. His beer went sprawling and spilled. The mug hit the floor and shattered. The bar fell silent. All eyes were on them.

"You better start talking right now, little man, and quickly," Charles growled. Jared was having trouble breathing. and his eyes were bulging. "Eeessssshahahhhhhhppgglgltt..." was all that he could manage to say.

Chuck dropped him to the table but didn't let go nor ease his intensity. "How long have you known?? Did you bother to tell Susan this!?"

"No... I... couldn't..." Jared wheezed, trying to breathe, his hands working on loosening Charles' grip.

"You piece of shit." Charles let him go, turned, and ran out of the bar.

Jared rolled off of the table and fell to his hands and knees. He was gasping for air. Stumbling forward. he tried to follow him.

He managed to squeak out one word.

"Wait!"

# CHAPTER THIRTY

SUSAN COULDN'T SLEEP. Her mind was racing. What had just happened? After the attack, she and Dimitri unceremoniously dumped Tanaka into the dumpster and left to go back to his place. After a heated but brief discussion on this crass decision, the logic of this move was this: This was a frontier town, and he wouldn't be discovered for some time, if at all when his remains hit the incinerator. They did not want the police involved or the public scrutiny. Susan argued that he had a family and that they needed to do the right thing. Dimitri argued that it would have been a complete and utter fiasco. Did she want that? The publicity would have been a nightmare. Still, as she reluctantly agreed, it did not sit well with her.

All garbage was automated. Not a soul would even look out back in the alley. The robot truck would come and pick up the dumpster, empty its contents into the back of its payload area and then crush it. When it hit the depot, it would be reduced to its atom structure, sorted, and then distributed to the 3D printers of the area. Tanaka would either be a printed steak or a table. It all depended on which machine used his molecules first.

The way that Dimitri shot him in the head so calmly and coolly, like he was turning off a light, was on her mind as well. She had long felt that he was not who he said he was. It was a nagging feeling that she couldn't prove or place her finger on. He was just too good-looking to be doing the job he was doing. He could have been a model, for crying out loud.

As she lay in Dimitri's bed thinking about the evening, he softly snored next to her. He seemed utterly unaffected by the evening's affairs. Exhaustion finally overcame her, most likely helped by the alcohol, and she drifted off.

It was there again, floating in the middle of the room in the lotus position. Its big almond-shaped eyes were open and looking at Susan. At least, she thought that they were. They were black and bottomless, those eyes. It had a slight smile on its face. A smile as much as its thin mouth could produce. Susan noticed that she was also in the lotus position and floating a few inches off the floor. She met his gaze, and she was totally calm and at peace. Being with it in these situations always did that. Her heart rate slowed, as did her breathing. Every muscle in her body was relaxed, even her shoulders.

Slowly they spun around each other, and the walls began to dissolve. Imperceptibly pinpoints of light started to appear all around them. Galaxies began to glow, planets spun, moons orbited, suns blazed, comets passed by, and asteroids crossed at random angles. The floor was gone now, along with the ceiling. Susan felt complete and utter cosmic consciousness. She was one with everything. She knew everything was connected; she could feel it in her soul.

Suddenly without warning, Fetu spoke softly and kindly.

"We are glad that you survived the attack of the others." It said as it spun slowly.

"The others? He was Japanese. Do you consider them 'others'?" Susan asked.

"No, Tanaka-san was not an 'other'. He was an unfortunate soul controlled by the Grays. Many times we tried to intervene, to save him, but to no avail. His mind was weak, corrupted by an insatiable appetite for exploration and greed. His life was a tragedy." Fetu slowly blinked. It seemed to take an eternity for Susan.

"I am so sorry to hear that. His death was needless." Susan said without emotion.

"Yes, it could have been avoided. He was sent to murder you because of what the Grays have feared for millennia." He sighed.

"What is that?" Susan asked, looking deep into its eyes. She could see herself in them. Stars swirled behind her. Supernova exploded.

"You," Fetu said, blinking its eyes slowly again.

"Me?" Susan was shocked.

"Yes, Susan, as we have told you before, you are uniquely special. Tonight we will give you a gift beyond imagining. We can no longer reside in an orb, waiting and doing nothing. We will give you the ability to heal your planet. We will give you the ability to travel the stars. We will give you the key to solving world hunger and homelessness. The orb that is in our tower will unite all of your people and bring about a new era in human history. There will be no want, no starvation, no more wars, no more haves and have-nots. Free energy to all." Fetu fell silent, and they rotated about each other; finally Susan spoke.

"Why do the Grays fear me?" She asked.

"Because the system you live in was created by them in accordance with keeping humans slaves, as cattle. They don't want you to evolve. They do not want you to prosper. They have no compassion, only scientific outcomes. They genetically removed compassion and feelings from their DNA. To them, it was... superfluous. Feelings got in the way." Once again, the age-old blink. It looked at her expectantly.

Susan floated in silence for a while, contemplating the truth of this. The wackadoos were right, after all. There had been beings - Grays - abducting us, meddling in our governments, creating wars. It had to stop. And now it sounded like it could; this orb would somehow break us free of their evil influence.

"How do I get the orb, and once I have it, what do I do with it?" Susan asked.

"You must enter the Gamma state on your own. You must not use the machine. It has to be pure thought." It put its long finger to its forehead and pressed it in a symbolic gesture.

Susan thought about this for a few seconds. Her mind raced. Fetu broke her chain of thought.

"Have you been practicing your meditations?" He asked.

"Yes, I have. I no longer need the machine to help my brain achieve gamma rays." She answered.

"This is most excellent. We have sensed your presence on more than one occasion, and we noticed the frequency is increasing. We feel that you are ready." A very faint smile hinted at the edges of Fetu's mouth.

"Ready for what?" Susan asked.

"To enter the Tower, to claim your birthright. To set your species free from bondage. To finally free yourselves from the Grays. You are fulfilling the prophecy..."

Susan cut Fetu off.

"*Whoa!* Hold on there. What did you say? Don't give me that chosen-one bull! I want no part of that."

"Calm young one, calm. Poor choice of words. Let us just say that we... "predicted" your emergence." His hand was raised, palm toward her to bring her back.

"All societies have a single individual that, for whatever reason, rises to the top, awakens, and sees clearer. You just happened to be that person. We've been waiting for you." Fetu reached out its hand to Susan in a gesture of calm.

"That is a pretty heavy thing to be laying on someone... I don't want it." Susan said softly. She couldn't look at it.

"That's why it has to be you. Those that seek power seldom deserve it. Their egos always get in the way. This is your crossroads, Susan, do you accept this responsibility, or do you walk away?" He looked at her unblinkingly, expressionless.

Susan was quiet for a long time. They both spun through the nothingness of space around each other slowly. Time had no meaning here. She closed her eyes. Took a deep breath and let it out slowly. She had never backed down from a challenge in her life. This was a chance to change everything. She had to try at least.

Opening her eyes, she looked directly into the depths of Fetu's eyes.

"I accept this mission." She said with a military edge. She sat up straighter.

Silently he reached forward with his long index finger and pressed it to her forehead. It burned, and a bright light blinded Susan. It felt like every cell of her body was exploding with pain and pleasure. A primal scream built up from the depths of her soul and finally worked its way out of her mouth.

---

Before he knew what was happening, Dimitri was on his feet with his gun in his hand. Susan was sitting up, panting, hands on her forehead.

"GREGORI RASPUTIN!" he cursed.

"What is the *matter*, woman?" Dimitri panted out.

Susan took a moment to catch her breath. She needed a minute to process. She slowly lowered her hands. Dimitri carefully lowered his weapon, not taking his eyes off her.

"By all that is unholy, what is that on your forehead?" Dimitri hissed. His finger was pointed at her head.

Susan's hand went back up and felt a small but distinct jewel. It was warm and cool at the same time. It was pulsing; she could feel it ever so gently.

"It's glowing." Dimitri breathed. His voice was a whisper.

Susan's breath was normal now. A calmness that she had never felt in her life swept over her. Everything made sense to her. The cosmos' confusion and the complexity seemed so simple and direct to her now. She looked at Dimitri for a long time, taking him in objectively. For the first time in his life, he was uncomfortable. He felt exposed. Raw.

Susan spoke clearly and succinctly.

"I must go now."

# CHAPTER THIRTY-ONE

CHARLES BURST into Susan's shack, not bothering to knock, hoping to catch Dimitri in some sinister, dastardly deed. Instead, he was greeted by an empty room. Even the socks and discarded underwear seem unaffected by his grand entrance. Jared came up behind him, winded, and tried to look around him. Charles barely fit through the doors here as it was. Charles entered and called out.

"Suze, you here?!" he bellowed.

No response; she wasn't in the bathroom either. Charles spun on his heel and moved toward the door. Jared was in the way, and Charles swept him aside like a piece of paper in the wind.

"Get out of my way, Benedict Arnold," he grunted under his breath, and he was out of the door, headed to the research lab by the base of the tower.

While he was on his butt, Jared shouted after Chuck.

"She's probably with Dimitri at his shack!"

Charles made no indication that he heard or cared. All he cared about was getting to Susan. Every fiber of his being was bent on it. He wasn't going to lose another sister. Not on his watch. He did heed Jared's advice, which in his rage, seemed to be the most logical place to look next. He finally had his reason to grab Dimitri and crush him into a little ball and toss him away over his shoulder. His justice was going to be swift and final. Dimitri was over.

Jared was on his feet and was brushing himself off as he tried to keep up with Chuck. "You know, for a big guy, you move fast!"

Charles ignored this too. At times his augs came in handy, and this was one of them. His new legs didn't tire as easily and allowed him to move like a cheetah. He steamed forward, hell-bent, towards Dimitri's shack.

He burst into this shack unannounced as well. Hitting the door with his shoulder, he didn't break his stride. The door didn't stand a chance. Coming off its hinges, it slid forward, standing up until it hit the bed, going end over end. Charles' eyes were on fire by now, and he was ready to pummel Dimitri into nonexistence - for hiding who he was from Susan, for misleading her, and who knew what other devious plans he had. Charles stood in the middle of the room, panting. No Susan, no Dimitri. He could feel the burning rising from deep within.

Where were they? Damnit.

Jared caught up, this time totally out of breath and sweating.

"Honestly man, are you an android or something? You are not human." he panted.

"I'm an aug, you idiot." Charles retorted, at his wit's end and fed up with this clown.

"Oh..." was all that Jared could muster. His hands were on his knees. He seriously thought he was going to hurl.

"She's got to be at the research lab," Chuck said as he headed out the door.

"Holy Hanna..." Jared said, still not having caught his breath. Somehow he managed to get his legs to move, even though they felt like jelly.

"Wait!" he managed to pant out as he stumbled forward.

---

Denise had been following them when they left "The Cooler." It was a challenge. Good thing she never let up on her training. She was in phenomenal shape and could tail Charles, even though he moved like a gazelle chased by a lioness. Tonight, she was that lioness, and Charles was her prey.

She had seen the big one pick up the little one by the collar and pull him over the table just before leaving with the bartender. She hadn't been interested in these two, but the commotion caught her eye. She was mulling over stalking Susan and Dimitri back to his shack but was now pleased to have her nasty way with the barkeep, Jason. As they rushed past her, she stopped in her tracks.

"Everything ok?" Jason asked.

He was completely confused by her total lack of forward motion.

Denise sighed.

"Sorry love, duty calls." With that being said, she kissed him on the cheek and was off.

# CHAPTER THIRTY-TWO

SUSAN ARRIVED at the research shack at the base of the tower. Dimitri was silently following her. She hadn't said a word to him since telling him about her dream. She had simply started to walk. She made her way directly to her station and sat in the lotus position in front of it. The hieroglyphs on the wall before her began to dance and hum. The gem in her forehead became white hot and glowed with a brilliant light. Dimitri had a hard time looking at her. She was awash in a sea of cosmic rays. Was she floating above the ground? He couldn't tell, but he'd be damned if she wasn't. This was the moment he had been waiting for; all the scheming and lying was finally coming together. And by Gregorio, it was about time. He didn't know how much longer he could be nice to this woman; the time to kill her was close.

Susan's hair was alive as it moved and swayed in the zero-G she was experiencing. She couldn't feel the ground anymore and knew she was levitating. Her entire body was alive with electricity. This was better than any lovemaking she had ever experienced. She could feel that the energy of the whole universe was channeling through her and culminating in her forehead. The gem was pulsing very deeply now, and she knew it would be released soon. She took in a very long, deep sustained breath, held it for a second, and then with all she had, she let it go. A stream of pure energy emitted from the bindi jewel in her head. Her third eye was awake and conscious. It hit the side of the tower directly on the writing. The hieroglyphs moved to the sides and formed an oblong oval, taller than wide. Slowly the ivoriness of the building began to fade, and an entrance appeared in its place.

Dimitri was taking all of this,, in a state of awe despite himself. He had never seen the likes of it, and every hair on his body was standing at attention. Susan was glowing so brightly now he was having a hard time seeing her. There was a low thrumming that he couldn't quite hear but felt in his bones. Dimitri thought it might shake him apart. He witnessed the beam coming out of her forehead and hitting the side of the tower. He saw the door to the tower open and blackness darker than a quantum singularity inside. He shuddered.

When it was over, Susan was standing in front of the opening. Her hair was still moving, and it reminded him of a hydra. She was clothed in a pure white aura that seemed to shimmer and move in a breeze that did not exist for him.

"Susan..." he whispered. She was more beautiful than any woman he had ever laid eyes upon before. She was a goddess. She didn't seem to hear him. She slowly moved forward into the entrance and was gone. Dimitri could not see into the opening, yet it remained. It had become deafeningly quiet, and he was alone in the room. His heart ached, and he was confused and suddenly felt very alone and small.

He called her name again.

"Susan."

"Susan!" louder this time. No response, just silence. He approached the door cautiously, gun in hand. He didn't know what to expect. Where did she go? He couldn't see a damn thing in there. It was pitch black. What was that feeling he was feeling? Fear? No, he had never felt that before. Slowly, he made his way over to the blackness. He reached his hand in with the gun, and it seemed to disappear. What sorcery was this? He quickly pulled it back out, and his hand was thankfully still attached to his torso; he breathed a sigh of relief.

He stood motionless for some time. The silence was deafening. This was the moment to act, but he hesitated. Finally, after what seemed like an eternity, he took a deep breath, stepped in, and was gone.

Charles came bursting into the science lab. Equipment was everywhere, like a tornado had swept through. He frantically searched the room with his eyes looking for Susan. He had to find her; he was in a state of panic. Where in the hell was she?

Jared stumbled in and tripped on a cable on the floor. He tried to catch himself, but his legs were made of silly putty by this time, and he sprawled forward onto his face. He slid a few feet, an oscilloscope ending his journey with a thud. He sat up, rubbing his head where a significant lump was setting up camp. It was going to be a dozy. Charles was standing in front of a black opening in the side of the tower in complete silence. His hands dangled by his side, and he was dumbfounded.

Jared came up beside him and rubbed his knot. It was pretty tender. "Do you think she went in there?" he said.

"I am afraid so..." he was in a state of shock.

The hieroglyphs on the edge of the door danced and swam, moving in a circle around the blackness. Charles reached out to touch them, and he felt a static charge.

Jared had moved over to the data table and cleared off the debris. He punched in the security code to bring up the twenty-four-hour holographic surveillance feed. It was unique because it produces a three-dimensional image you can move around in post-production. His eyes grew wide as the screen began to glow brightly on his face.

"Uhhh... you better come see this," he said to Charles slowly.

"What is it?" Charles was beyond frustrated and angry by now; he didn't have time for Jared's games. He was at his wit's end. He turned and looked at him and was taken aback by the expression on Jared's face. It was like he saw a ghost. He moved toward the monitor.

"What the...?"

It was all Charles could manage. He had arrived at Jared's shoulder just in time to see Susan glowing and entering the entrance. They stood there for a few moments in silence. Neither couldn't believe what they had just seen. A few minutes later, they could see Dimitri follow her in with a gun.

"Son of a..." Charles was moving before Jared knew what was happening. Dimitri looked up to see the leg of Charles slipping into the blackness. He was alone. Dimitri knew what he had to do, but he couldn't move. It was his chance to blow this building and everything in it all to hell. All he had to do was step inside and detonate the vest. All his misery would be over. And yet... he had grown fond of them, even though they hadn't accepted him. He was still alone. Always and again. Curiosity got the better of him, and he moved toward the emptiness on the wall. He stood in front of it, frozen. He knew if he entered, there would be no turning back, that it was the end. He closed his eyes and stepped forward.

---

Denise rolled into the room like a panther, ready for anything. But there was... Nothing. The only thing that greeted her was the soft buzz of electronics and a very low vibration that made her back teeth rattle. The only thing playing was a holo-recorder. She made her way over to the device, pressed the rewind button, and watched the events of the evening unfold.

"That little minx. She figured it out..." she whispered. She saw Dimitri enter the tower a few minutes after Susan. His gun was drawn. A few moments after that, she saw the other two buffoons enter. Nonplussed, she moved toward the opening and pulled her Ruger out. She cocked it, and without hesitation; she walked in sideways, gun at the ready by her shoulder.

The door closed a few seconds later. No trace of it having ever existed was apparent. The low humming had stopped. All that was left was the beeping and humming of the empty lab.

# CHAPTER THIRTY-THREE

SUSAN slowly and purposefully made her way to the tower's center. Dimitri followed closely behind her. She seemed to be gliding over the surface of the mirrored alabaster floor. He could not discern any movement of her feet below her all-encompassing aura. It pulsated with a life all its own. She seemed oblivious to all around her; her mind focused on a single goal. The space they were in was vast, almost like another dimension; it seemed bigger than its outside would suggest. There was no one inside, the emptiness seeming to suck the sound out of the air. What struck Dimitri the most was that there was absolutely nothing in the tower. Nothing. It was just a vast, cavernous space.

Susan was making her way to a tube in the center of the expansive room. It was clear and extended upwards to a vanishing point. He couldn't make out the end of it; it seemed to disappear into the distance. She stopped in front of it and placed her left palm on it. She seemed calm and purposeful, with no hesitation. Susan moved forward and was suddenly through the glass, on the inside of the tube. She turned and looked at him but didn't seem to see him. Her expression was empty, and there was no recognition there. She looked through him. It made him self-conscious, something he rarely felt. She ascended up the tube, apparently in thin air. He watched her go up, and then she was gone.

When he finally reached the tube, there was no opening. He touched the side with his open left palm, and to his surprise, he fell through. Catching himself, he stood upright and could feel a force pulling him upwards. He relaxed and went with it. As he ascended, he could see Charles, and lagging far behind was Jared, both making their way toward the tube.

"I should have killed you sooner, Jared. Now you are truly being a pain in the ass," he said softly to himself. He thought that he would have to murder the giant as well, even though he had respect for him. He knew he was a boy scout and would just get in the way. All that mattered was what was at the top of this tower. Dimitri took a breath. His revenge could wait, but he would have it. The technology that awaited him could not wait. Susan would lead him right to it, and he would take the artifact and dispose of her. Everything was coming together nicely.

He watched the two of them some distance apart. As he ascended the tube, Dmitri saw Jared was having trouble keeping up, bringing up the rear. Jared was pointing upward at Dimitri, yelling. He could see Charles look up and then run toward the tube. Charles was fast, leaving Jared even further behind. He might catch up to him, possibly, but not before he killed Susan and took what she had and then shot each in turn as they left the top of the shaft. Clean and simple. He loved his focus on purpose during stress. It was the best part of the job.

---

"Look! He's up there!"

Jared shouted, pointing at Dimitri.

Charles looked up and saw Dimitri floating up, gun in hand, held high. He must be following Susan, and the gun did not look cocked in protection; it looked aggressive. Charles broke into a full sprint and left Jared in the dust. He knew he was hitting around fifty kilometers per hour; he had his buddy track him when he first got his new legs. Usain Bolt had nothing on him. He reached the tube and abruptly stopped, skidding into place. The tube was sealed. No indication of a seam, door, hinge, or opening.

"Dammit! I am too late. There's no way in" He watched Dimitri fade into the distance above, cursing his slow body. He stood there in complete and utter defeat. He had failed Susan; he had lost another sister. He knew that Dimitri would kill her; he just knew it.

Jared limped up to the tube and went to rest his hand on it to catch his breath. He fell right into it. Charles reached in and picked him up.

"You're a freaking genius," he said as he stepped into the tube, and they both floated up together. Not fast enough for Charles, but there was still hope that he could destroy Dimitri before he touched Susan.

Denise strolled into the atrium just in time to see Laurel and Hardy floating up the tube. She made her way over and examined the tube. She was in no hurry, but she wasn't dawdling either. She was on her own timeline, and whatever happened would work out in her favor. It usually did. She was just curious as to how all of this would turn out. Her best guess was that Dimitri would take the prize from Susan and shoot her, and then he would probably end up killing the other two fools. She understood Dimitri's burning need to kill Jared for slaying Marco. She applauded Dimitri's restraint. He was always in control. It was sexy.

With her left hand raised, she walked up to the tube and strolled into it without missing a step. She looked up as she floated to the top. As she ascended, she checked her Ruger one last time to make sure that there was a bullet in the chamber. Can't be too careful in these situations. Nonchalantly looking at her watch, she wondered how all this drama would play out.

She was quite sure that it would be infinitely entertaining.

# CHAPTER THIRTY-FOUR

SUSAN REACHED the top of the tube and floated out of it onto an open area. The view was spectacular. Two miles up and clear skies. The top of the tower was now gone and open to the space above it. She could see for miles. In the center was a brilliant glowing orb made of pure white. Electricity bounced around it. It was so white it seemed to be made of light itself. She made her way over to it. It was approximately the size of a volleyball. It spun slowly in its central chSusan, hovering above a platform in the center of the veranda. Just looking at it made her feel warm and fuzzy all over. Standing beside it was Fetu; he shimmered in the sun. Susan could see through him. His hands were interlaced in front of him, and he had a broad smile upon his diminutive frame.

"Welcome, Susan." He said. "I see that you have accepted your higher self."

"Yes, I have. I see the truth of everything now. I see the interconnectedness of the universe. I see how we are all one and never alone." She was slowly moving towards him and the orb. Her hair was still alive and her aura flowed around her like silk on a warm autumn day. The breeze at the top of the tower was unusually warm for this height and latitude.

"Then you are ready to receive great knowledge and insight that will serve all humans," Fetu said, spreading its arms in a grand gesture.

"Yes, I am." She reached the dais and slowly put her hands into the field and around the orb. She took it, gently holding it aloft as she removed it from its chSusan. Her hair seemed even more alive than before. Her aura seemed to swirl around her faster. Her eyes began to glow. Her bindi looked to be on fire. Holding the orb, she slowly rose above the floor three inches. The aura around her of soft white light grew even brighter. She was emitting a low humming sound of 432 hertz.

"I'll take that, thank you," Dimitri said, pointing his gun at Susan.

Susan hovered above the floor. She didn't say a word. Dimitri circled around so he could face her and the entrance, not wishing to be caught off guard by Charles and Jared when they came through the tube.

"The orb is pretty. And your friend is quite unusual." Dimitri said. "Is he the one that's been guiding you? The one you have been dreaming about?"

Susan remained silent. She seemed to be staring into the distance, not focusing on anything. Fetu spoke.

"I know who you are, and you have no place here. Your kind is finished. The orb will change everything. If you shoot her, the orb will go back to its original place, and this tower will lock down. Your government will never have it. You will be trapped here." Fetu spoke utterly emotionless.

"Whatever, Dobby." said Dimitri, waving the gun, "Hand it over, princess. Now."

Susan continued to float, unaffected by Dimitri's presence.

---

Charles reached the top of the tower and saw Dimtri pointing a gun at Susan. He then saw Susan, and his jaw dropped. Dimitri looked at him immediately. Charles froze and took in the sight of her floating and glowing. She was gorgeous. Shaking his head out of his stupor, he stepped forward into a sprinting stance. He was going to charge Dimitri. Damn the bullets.

"Hold it right there, hero. One more step, and I put a bullet in her head." Dimitri warned.

He stopped dead in his tracks. Charles was cursing himself for not having a gun.... He just didn't believe in them. He was seriously questioning that conviction at the moment. Behind him, Jared finally made it to the party and silently walked around to Dimitri's left.

"What in the hell..." Jared gasped.

"That's enough eco-terrorist, pretty boy. Your time is up. No one will leave this platform alive, least of all you. I have been waiting for this for some time," said Dimitri, smiling. He hadn't been this happy in ages. As soon as Susan handed him the orb, he would start shooting. Marco would be pleased.

A news drone appeared to pop up out of nowhere. It hovered approximately fifteen feet away from the platform, slowly circling the Diaz.

Good, the world could watch, Dimitri thought, he didn't care.

Dimitri continued, "Well, what's it going to be, Susan? Which friend do you want me to shoot first? Charles? Jared? Fetu? You have till the count of three, and then people start dying."

Still, she floated in a trance, unconcerned about the problems of the world. She seemed to be downloading information. She was slowly talking to herself in a sing-song voice. A change from the humming she had been doing a few minutes ago, but still seemingly oblivious to everything external.

"Not so fast, Dimitri." Denise strolled off the tube platform like a cat with her Ruger pointed at him. "I have had enough of your games. Put the gun down, or I'll put *you* down."

"Well, it seems we have what you Americans call a 'Mexican stand-off.'" Dimitri laughed. This just kept getting better and better. It was like one of the old westerns he so loved and enjoyed. He was living one now and couldn't be happier.

"You know what?!" Jared yelled. "I have had enough of all of this and all of you!" He was boldly walking around the edge of the platform towards Susan and Fetu. He had his jacket off, and his vest was now visible for all to see. He had the trigger in his hand, his thumb hovering over a red button. For the life of him, he didn't know why he hadn't pushed it already. He was sick of all of them and their drama.

No one said a word. The wind howled through the group. Susan's aura flowed, her hair danced, and the orb crackled. She continued to hum. Charles half expected a tumbleweed to roll by and a buzzard to screech. Everyone was frozen in place.

"Yeah, it's what you think it is. It's a Quantum bomb. Say goodbye to your neutrinos." Jared smiled wryly. He held the trigger up on high in case they missed it.

"You are such an asshole," Charles said. "I can't believe I was actually starting to like you. First Dimitri, and now you? Dude. Seriously?"

"Whatever, Mr. high and mighty with superior genetics. I hate guys like you, born the best, and look down on the rest. What did you do to deserve it? Nothing. Simply born privileged." Jared raised the trigger higher. "I am in control here. This is it for you, for all of you. One press of this trigger and every atom will be ripped apart in your body."

"You're bluffing!" Dimitri shouted.

"Am I?!" Jared had a crazed look in his eyes. He lifted the trigger higher.

In the distance, a helicopter could be heard. Once the first news drone entered, the news spread like wildfire and a second drone appeared just a few minutes later. This caught his attention, but Jared didn't care either way. It was good that these events were being recorded and televised worldwide. The top of the tower disappearing must have caused quite a stir in the shantytown below.

Jared turned to Susan.

"And you! Not giving me the time of day, thinking you were better than me. Putting me down, laughing at me behind my back. Rubbing Dimitri in my face. Mocking me..." he spat. He was crying now, freely. He knew these were his last moments.

Susan was aware of all around her but made no indication that she was. She continued to absorb the orb's infinite information.

Charles took this moment of distraction to move. As Jared was yelling at Susan, he exploded from a standstill. All his will was bent on catching Jared's hand and stopping the pressing of that button. Jared turned at the last minute to see a blur of speed. Charles hit him like a freight train, and he could feel Jared's ribs crack like dry twigs. All of the air left him. The momentum of the hit took them both over the edge.

Demetrius took this opportunity to spin around and take a shot at Denise. She was quick, and she rolled as he pulled the trigger. His bullet missed her by mere inches, ricocheted off the pedestal, and caught Fetu in the head. It went right through him. Fetu seemed unfazed by the assault.

Denise came out of her roll and, on one knee, put three bullets into Dimitri's chest. He fell to his knees and looked at her. He wobbled for a second. Dark blood came out of his mouth, and he fell face forward with a thud.

Denise ran over to where Fetu was standing, seemingly unaffected by the events around him. She tried to touch his head where the bullet had entered. It went through to the wall. Was he a hologram? She shuddered. She whispered, "How?"

"I am so sorry, my child. You must be Denise. I am not truly here. I am just a projection of the tower. I gave it my consciousness eons ago." It said consolingly.

Denise didn't know what to say, her head was spinning, and she was dizzy. She reached out her hand instinctively to Fetu's hand, and it passed through thin air. It smiled at her reassuringly. "It seems we have company." It said as it pointed to the sky. Denise turned to look and saw a point far away. Black Hawk? She wasn't sure. She turned back to talk to Fetu, but he was gone.

A helicopter was in the distance and growing steadily. It was a gunship. Would they open fire and join the fray? Denise didn't know, but was at Susan's side, gun ready to defend her as she continued to float and absorb the orb's energy through her bindi.

Suddenly it stopped, and Susan collapsed to the deck of the tower. She landed on her feet, first falling to her side. The orb fell, too, and landed beside her with a dead thud. It did not bounce, nor did it move or move from the place it landed. Rolling onto her butt, she reached over and picked it up. She cradled it in her lap and stroked it, not saying a word. Her aura was gone.

Suddenly the wind picked up tremendously and blew her hair all around her face. Denise looked up and saw the gunship hovering above the tower in front of them. Denise trained her Ruger on the pilot, waiting for a hail of minigun fire. It did not come as the vehicle made its way to the side of them and landed.

"Hop in ladies, I'm your ride out of here!" Jeb's voice boomed over the microphone.

# CHAPTER THIRTY-FIVE

CHARLES AND JARED tumbled end over end down the side of the tower. Two miles is a long way to fall, approximately forty seconds. They didn't know this, but it certainly gave them time to think about their situation. Twelve seconds in, they had already hit terminal velocity. Charles had a death grip on Jared's trigger hand and he squeezed it so hard he heard the bones in Jared's wrist crack. He cried out in pain.

"I hate you!" He screamed at Charles. "Why won't you let me die?"

"That's gonna happen soon enough, just not your way!" Charles yelled back.

Charles began to feel the side of the tower against him. It was a gentle slope to the bottom that gradually flattened to the ground. He thought for a split second that he wouldn't die after all. He tried to position himself so that he would slide down the side and reduce his rate of falling. Jared wasn't making it easy. He struggled to regain control and press the button with his other hand. Jared knew he only had a limited amount of time before they struck the Earth.

Charles knew that if they didn't slow down, they would still hit the buildings at the bottom surrounding the tower at one hundred and fifty miles per hour. Not good. He knew his augs would be able to slow them down from terminal velocity if he could just get his boots flat on the side of the tower.

"Listen!" Charles yelled at Jared. "It's not too late! We can survive this!"

"I. Don't. Give. A. Shit. Let go!" Jared grunted through the pain. He tried to reach the button.

"No!" Charles yelled.

Charles had Jared's other wrist in his other hand. He brought his knee up as hard as he could right into Jared's groin. He felt Jared's coccyx give way with a loud snap. He whimpered. The pain proved too much for him, and he passed out. Charles grabbed Jared around the waist and turned him around. He then grabbed the trigger and held it tightly away from Jared's reach in case he regained consciousness.

The side of the building was racing by now enough to cause friction. His back was warming. He planted his feet as flat as he could. He pushed. The force was tremendous. His math was weak, but he figured they were doing about one hundred and forty miles per hour. His aug legs and knees strained under the tension but held. The soles of his boots squealed with friction. They started to smoke. He was slowing down ever so slightly. He could see that the buildings underneath him were getting larger rather quickly. There was a street below them, an opening! If he could just steer himself towards it, they might just slide on their butt down the boulevard and not slam into the shanty town shops.

He barely missed the food shack to his right; he had to lean on his side. He still had Jared, not wanting to let go for fear that the vest might detonate on its own. They hit the dirt road at about one hundred miles an hour, probably less. He wasn't sure of his speed, but his buttocks were on fire, his pants were gone and his skin was going with them... He held fast. The road rash was going to hurt later. It was like hitting asphalt after falling off a motorcycle doing eighty. Happened to his father.

Unfortunately for them, this was not a thru street. A fruit stand was right in the middle of it. He braced himself for impact. Fortunately, it was not a solid building but stacked crates and a cart. Charles picked up his feet and bent his knees, hoping his aug legs would cushion the blow and withstand the impact. They hit the stand at a good sixty miles per hour. Shop owners and customers dove out of the way. Crates exploded, and fruits and vegetables went flying like a tossed fruit salad.

Everything went dark.

# CHAPTER THIRTY-SIX

SUSAN CRADLED the dead orb in her lap as the helicopter raced her to the medic station at the United States Antarctic Embassy. After a few moments, she wrapped the orb in a blanket and tucked it beside her. Susan turned and looked out of the side of the copter. The tower was fading in the distance. She knew she had lost Charles when he tackled Jared, but that he died a hero and saved the town. She wept.

Denise sat across from her and watched. She had the helicopter headphones on. After a moment's consideration, she turned to the pilot.

"Who in the hell are you, anyway?" she yelled into the mic.

"Names Jeb, me, and Susan go way back."

"Is that so?"

"Yep! What is your name?"

"Denise." She thought he was handsome as hell. He had that midwestern draw and an older rugged look to him. A silver fox, so to speak. The thick mustache and beard stubble just added to the charm. And his voice was deep and strong. "It's a pleasure to meet you, Jeb," Denise yelled back.

Jeb turned around and took Denise all in. She looked fantastic in her all-black jumpsuit. She knew it. "It's a real pleasure to meet you too, Denise." He winked.

He turned back around and turned a few dials, taking readings and adjusting as they flew. "Not every day I get to give two lovely ladies a joy ride." He said to himself.

After some time, he turned around again.

"How is she doing?" Jeb asked.

"Still hasn't said a word," Denise responded. "At least her eyes aren't glowing anymore, and she's not floating."

Hell of a thing, Jeb thought. An ancient artifact in his 'copter, plus a celebrity scientist and a hired assassin; not a bad Tuesday after all. He never believed in any of that hogwash about extraterrestrials. HQ had briefed him on the situation. You just never knew what the day was going to bring. He had gotten the green light from his CO as soon as the top of the tower had suddenly disappeared. He thought it would never come. He ran to the Black Hawk he had under a tarp in the back of the bar's parking lot. Damn, it felt good to be back at the controls of this bird. He missed it.

He had radioed in that he was bringing them in and that, yes, indeed Virginia, there was a Santa Claus. Code for he had procured the orb. As soon as he touched down, men in white hazmat suits approached the craft. They took the orb from Susan without much protest from her. She was still in her catatonic state. A medic reached in and helped Susan out and into a wheelchair. Denise hopped out to get behind Susan and follow the men into the building, hands on the wheelchair.

"Well, take it from here, Ma'am!" one of them said over the din of the Black Hawk.

"Where are you taking her!?" Denise shouted over the whirling blades.

"For observation. Standard procedure in these situations. We will keep you apprised." He turned and wheeled Susan down the tarmac towards the hanger. Denise started to protest and follow but noticed two armed guards with submachine guns. They raised them and looked in her direction. She backed down.

"Hop in, Denise!" Jeb shouted. "Our work here is done. We'll be back to see her. I promise." he winked at her again.

Denise walked around, head down, and piled into the passenger seat. She put the headphones back on.

"So, what now?" She said to Jeb.

"Why don't we go back to my place for a drink?"

Denise was silent for a second. She saw the look in his eyes. "Why the hell not? I could use a stiff one!"

They both laughed as Jeb pulled back on the stick, and the craft lifted into the air.

---

Charles was on his stomach. The nanites were busy at work repairing the subcutaneous tissues of his butt and back. They were assisting in growth and repair. The doc said that in a week he would have the "butt of a newborn baby". In the bunk next to him was Jared in traction. Nanites were working on his wrist, ribs, and coccyx bones. Doc said a week for him too.

Forrest Gump was playing on the holoscreen in the background. "Lieutenant Dan! Ice Cream!" The irony of the scene was not lost on him. Charles didn't know if he could stomach a whole week with Jared. He contemplated killing him on more than one occasion. He just wouldn't stop whining. Through tears, he had told him for the millionth time that he was sorry. Charles ignored him. He wasn't ready to forgive him, not just yet.

The door to their room opened, and Nigel entered. He looked directly at Charles. Their eyes met and they acknowledged each other but were silent.

Jared lit up.

"You came," he said, his voice choking.

"Of course I did, you big dummy. As soon as your ribs snapped, I got the notice and hopped on a transport. I had a feeling you were in trouble." He looked at Jared with sympathy. "What was with the neutrino vest? Jesus man... W.T.F.? Seriously?" He whistled.

Jared looked away. "I was done with it all. I wanted to go out with a bang, no pun intended. I wanted to fuck this society in the ass. It didn't deserve the orb. It needed to die."

"Huh, past tense." Nigel looked pensive. After a brief moment, he said. "And now?"

"I dunno. Charles saved me in spite of what I was trying to do..."

"I didn't do it for you, Jared." Charles interrupted.

Jared continued, ignoring Charle's slight. "...and now you, my only friend, coming all this way to see me... makes me happy." Jared sniffed.

"Now don't get all mushy on me now. Just doing my job." Nigel flashed that winning smile of his.

"And how are you doing over there sir?" Nigel said to Charles.

"Just peachy keen," he grunted.

"Thank you for saving my friend's life," Nigel said. "You saved a lot of people that day."

"Whatever... I'm just doing my job. Certainly didn't do it for him. Any word on Susan? Where is she? Is she ok?" Charles had a worry in his voice.

"She is safe and sound recovering. You'll probably be able to see her when you get out with your new behind." Nigel smiled broadly, pleased at his own little pun.

"Hah, hah. Very funny." Charles said without humor.

One more butt joke, and he was going to start punching people.

# CHAPTER THIRTY-SEVEN

SUSAN WAS in the lotus position, floating in deep space. She spun slowly as she hummed an ohm mantra. Nebulas were all around her; stars were being born. Each one ignites with the promise of a new solar system, new planets, and new life. Something inside of her had changed. She was calmer and more centered than she had ever been in her life. She felt like she belonged, had a purpose, and was part of the universe.

The nebula in front of her started to simmer and sway. Slowly Fetu came into focus.

"I didn't know if I would ever see you again," Susan whispered.

"Oh, my child, I will always be with you. Now that the contents of the orb are with you, so am I." Susan reflected upon this.

"What about the orb? What should I do? We didn't have a chance to talk. I feel so lost." Susan's brow was deeply furrowed with worry.

"Do not worry about the orb. You don't need it anymore. It has changed you. You have a new purpose now." Fetu smiled gently.

"What purpose is that?" Susan asked.

"To lead the people of this planet to the next step of their evolution." It looked at her compassionately.

"Like a spiritual leader? We both know what happened to the last

Jewish person that tried to do that. No thank you. I'm allergic to nails." She said.

Fetu smiled. The humor was not lost on him.

"Not quite. The orb imparted to you all of its knowledge in the brief time that you were in contact with it. Think of yourself as more of a... scientific leader. You will invent some incredible things that will change the face of the Earth. You need to surround yourself with the best minds available."

They floated around each other in silence as Susan let this sink in.

"Take care, my child. All will be revealed in time. Be patient." He started to fade.

"Wait! I have so many more questions. Don't go!"

"I must."

"Will I see you again?" Susan was distraught.

"I will always be with you, my child. Namaste." and he was gone.

---

Susan slowly opened her eyes to reveal a room full of people. Charles was staring down at her. He was holding her hand.

"You're awake. How are you feeling?" There was genuine concern in his eyes.

Susan's eyes widened. "You're alive?!"

"Yes, it's a really good story I don't think I will ever get tired of telling." He smiled broadly. "I thought I lost you there, kiddo. You were in a coma for a pretty long time."

"I was? How long? I don't remember..." she trailed off.

"A little over a month. You were fine at first, but your condition started to deteriorate. At least that is what the doctors told us." Chuck squeezed her hand.

"After he got his shiny new ass, he hasn't left your side," Denise said.

"Huh, butt? What?" Susan was confused.

"I'll explain later over a beer." Charles blushed.

Susan sat up on her elbows. "The orb, where is the orb? I need it. I want it after all that's happened."

"It's gone," Nigel spoke this time. "So is the Tower, well, not gone but dead. It's just an empty shell now. The hieroglyphs disappeared."

"Who are you?" Susan asked, but before Nigel could answer, Jared cut in.

"I am sorry, Susan. I know that means the end of your research." Jared spoke. Susan looked at him with malice.

"And I am so sorry for everything else too... you know, trying to blow up Antarctica and all." He looked down and shuffled his feet like he was thirteen and in the principal's office.

"And trying to murder everyone. Why are you not in prison?" Susan hissed.

"MI-6 is the short answer," he replied. "I have to report back to them immediately. I begged them to let me apologize to you personally."

Susan remained silent. The silence was deafening. All she could see in her mind's eye was Charles going over the edge of the tower with him.

"Well, that was awkward!" Nigel said. "Let's get out of here. Nice to meet you finally Susan. I hope that you are feeling better." Nigel grabbed Jared by the arm and ushered him out of the room. The three of them looked at each other.

"Now what?" Denise asked.

"No orb?" Susan asked. "What happened to it?"

"That's just it," Denise responded in her thick Portuguese accent. "It never existed. At least according to the government. Every time we ask, they deny it."

Susan pondered this for a few seconds, then spoke.

" It doesn't matter. Fetu said that I didn't need it."

"He did? When?" Charles inquired. "I thought he was dead."

"Just a few moments ago. He appeared in my dreams I guess." Susan leaned back off her elbows, letting her head sink into the pillow.

"I thought we needed it for all of the information from his society." Charles rubbed his beard thoughtfully.

"According to him, it's all in here." Susan touched the bindi in the middle of her forehead.

"It suits you. It's kinda sexy." Denise teased. "Makes me wish I had one."

"They couldn't remove it. I already asked." Charles said. "Believe me, they *tried*. I guess they gave up."

Susan caressed it lightly. It was warm, and she could feel it pulsing ever so slightly.

"I know what I need to do." She finally said.

"What's that?" Denise asked.

"I need to get the hell out of here and get a drink, that's what." She smiled.

"Well, now, that's the smartest thing I have ever heard you say!" Denise seemed very pleased with this turn of events.

"I'll get your things," Charles said, heading out the door. He returned a few moments later to Susan and Denise, chatting about Dimitri. They abruptly stopped. Charles pretended not to notice. "Here you go. I'll wait outside while you get dressed. Meet you out there; well, head over to The Cooler for old time's sake." He walked out into the hall and closed the door behind him.

Susan looked at Denise. "We'll finish this conversation later, ok?" Denise nodded in agreement. This was going to take some time to hash out between them, and that was a girl's night with a bottle of wine. Maybe two, certainly not in a hospital room. They exited together, met Charles in the hallway, and started to make their way out.

They walked for a few moments, and Charles broke the silence.

"Hey, I have been wondering... do either of you scuba?"

# CHAPTER THIRTY-EIGHT

JARED SAT in Carol's office waiting room and was nervous. He didn't know what to expect. Was she going to chew him out? Was he going to jail or, worse, be executed for treason? His mind raced. He sat for quite a while, waiting for her to enter. The secretary looked his way occasionally, but he offered no solace either. He went back to his duties, seemingly content that Jared had not left yet.

Finally, the phone buzzed, and the secretary answered.

"Yes ma'am.... No, ma'am... Yes ma'am, immediately." he said in a deep baritone. He hung up the phone and looked at Jared.

"You can go in now, sir," was all he said. He went back to typing on his keyboard, not looking up.

Jared slowly made his way over to the double doors of her office and opened the right door, letting himself in. The director was at her desk, engrossed in something on her viewscreen. She did not acknowledge him.

He cleared his throat. She stopped typing. He immediately regretted that decision.

Finally, she looked up at him over her reading classes. Her dark brown eyes drilled into him. She deliberately took her glasses off and put

ROBERT FENWICK MAY, JR

them on the desk. He put his hand on the chair in front of her desk to sit down but stopped dead.

"Stand where you are, agent." She said in an icy tone.

Agent? Was he still an agent? His mind raced. Was he not about to be destroyed?

Carol rubbed her eyes, sighed, and then looked at Jared.

"What in the hell happened down there?"

Jared was at a loss for words; surely, she knew everything.

"Go on; I want to hear it from your lips."

"I lost it." was all he could muster.

"No shit..." she sighed. "Well, for better or worse, and for me, it's worse, believe me, you are my agent."

Jared had a very confused look but remained silent and readied himself for the attack.

"And the higher-ups feel that it was my fault and that I need to correct my oversight."

"I don't understand, ma'am."

"Shut up, Jared," she said slowly.

"Yes ma'am," he whispered and stood silently.

Carol took a deep breath. "You are to be trained. They feel that you would have performed better with the proper training, completing your mission, and bringing the artifact home. All you lacked was the emotional fortitude to do this. This can be trained. All double O's have this ability."

Jared breathed in an audible gasp.

"Trust me; I am just as shocked as you. Report to psych first thing tomorrow morning for an evaluation and then wait for further orders. Your training starts next week, double O." There was a tinge of sarcasm in her voice.

"Yes ma'am," Jared said and then stood there.

"You are dismissed, agent. You will report back to me within a year after you have completed your training for your first mission. Now get out of my sight."

Without a word, Jared turned and was gone.

Mi6 had completely lost its mind and this is not how Carol had foreseen her career going. At least he was handsome, fit the profile, and was tall. Maybe that's what they saw in him; those types of men seem to garner a certain type of respect wherever they go. He probably did look good in a tux. She shook herself out of her thought pattern, he was still a cold-blooded murderer, and she knew that was exactly what they saw in him. He was also a little psychotic. *And* he could be controlled and manipulated. But he was also dangerous to the extreme. Those types of men always came to a bad end.

She sat back in her chair, looked out of her window at the London skyline, and focused on the Eye. It was slowly spinning the way everything else does until it didn't anymore. The slow, inexorable movement of time. She reached forward to her cabinet to the side and pulled out a bottle of GlenDronach Single Malt and a glass. She pulled the cork and poured. Putting it up to her lips, she breathed in the scent and then slowly took a sip. It warmed her soul. She needed it after this turn of events.

Who knows, maybe she would get lucky, and he would get killed in the field...

# *EPILOGUE*

"JUST TAKE IT. Box it up and file it away." Dr. Johnson said defeatedly. He rubbed the skin of his balding black forehead in frustration.

"Are you sure, doc? Maybe we can run a few more tests? Shock it some more. I dunno, something, anything?" his assistant Jacob said, pushing his glasses up with his middle finger. "Beat it with a hammer?"

Dr. Johnson did not laugh. He was so excited to receive this ancient relic. All the funding he had received. All of the secrets it held that the American military could use. All of the papers he would write. All of the recognition, fame, and fortune was gone. It was just a useless paper weight now.

He wondered if it was even real. He saw the video; hell, the whole world saw how it picked that woman up and gave her the ability to defy gravity. She was *glowing* for crying out loud. Now, the orb seemed to have no magic left; it was just a curiosity. Not even that, it was just a ball of stone, nothing more. It wasn't even interesting enough to land in the collection of the Natural history museum in DC.

A Nobel prize in physics would have been nice, using its secrets to unlock the universe.

He sighed.

"No, we're done here. Dispose of it. Take it home for all I care."

"Really?"

"Yes, I will fill out all the necessary paperwork for you. Just get it out of my sight."

Jacob shrugged, picked it up, put it under his arm, and walked out of the lab and then the building. No one stopped him; he just had a ball of granite. He took his prize home and placed it on the mantle of his fireplace.

Later that night, it started to gently glow...

# ACKNOWLEDGMENTS

Nothing we do is in a vacuum. Nothing we do, we do alone or without influence from others. No human is an island. As I wrote this book, all I could think of was my mother and the life she did not have because of me. She was young and beautiful and academic. She did well in school and idolized Jackie O. She wanted to change the world. But, as life would have it, she became pregnant at the tender age of 18 and another path was laid before her. My parents chose to marry and have me, for which I am eternally grateful. Looking back as an adult, it must have been hard for my mother to watch her dreams of college fade. What would her life have been like without my emergence? Don't get me wrong. I know that she loved me and my sister dearly, but, there was a deep hurt in her that would come out occasionally, a frustration with her situation. Susan *is* her, as that was her name. I dedicated the book to the grand daughter she never met, my daughter Sam. She lives on in my daughter in ways that I cannot explain to her but see and feel daily. I dated a research scientist from Hopkins as I wrote this and wondered if my mother could have been a pHd. She was tremendously helpful in fleshing out the main character and the female psyche. For that I owe her a debt of gratitude. I saw in her what my mother could have been given a different chance in life. My mother did go on to become the manager of the bank she worked for, of which all of us were immensely proud. She was also an avid reader. She read and collected every Steven King novel, one of my favorite authors. Her passion for reading was contagious. I caught that bug. She passed more than 30 years ago and that amazes me. Not a day goes by to this day that I don't think of her. At this point in my life, my only regret is that I discovered my passion for writing so late in life and that she didn't get a chance to be my biggest fan. I like to think that she is standing behind me, reading what I write over my shoulder. Our mothers hold tremendous sway over us. So, my acknowledgement is for her and all the other mothers of this world.

Thank you mom, for every thing, especially my life.

I love you.

# ABOUT THE AUTHOR

Robert has been a fan of science fiction since he can remember. At the tender age of 10 he saw Star Wars. He went home excited to learn to fly space ships, because in his young mind, there was no way that could have been faked. Even though as he grew he discovered the truth, it still didn't sour his love of the genre. It fueled it, wanting to learn everything, watch every movie and read everything he could get his hands on. Profoundly influenced by the Incal, he dreamed of writing his own book. He currently loves teaching children with learning differences high school algebra. He also likes to play the bass and create art.

www.adeventureartist.online

facebook.com/robertfenwickmayjr

twitter.com/AdventureArt67

instagram.com/adventureartistinc

patreon.com/robertfenwickmayjr

pinterest.com/robertfenwickmayjr